The Peng[illegible]

'Origins'

By *Darren Greg Johnson*

The Penguins Theory Origins

Foreword:

This book is a shortened version of a larger novel which is titled ‘The Penguins Theory’ (due for release by Autumn 2017, me hopes). There are several reasons why I wanted to bring out a shortened version; firstly, I want to give the reader a feel for how ‘The Penguins Theory’ came about, how it grew and so forth (and also what its all about). So without further ado, here go’s....

I have had a bit of a difficult life (as many people, who grew up in ‘less privileged places’, from the start of ‘civilization’, have also had). When I was 24 years old I decided to join the Army, I had tried to move away before, - to make a fresh start and do something worthwhile with my life - but after several failed attempts, joining up seemed the only possible way to improve things. I was not particularly strong, had no money and had little friends or family who lived anywhere more 'prosperous'; things were not looking rosy from the outset, and so ultimately, my 'fresh starts' failed. I had much difficulty joining the Armed forces as I am very much a pacifist and gentle natured person at heart and the thought of being put in a position where I may have to seriously harm or even kill another human being was very difficult for me to reason with. However after several years of fighting with my heart and being totally frustrated and broken hearted at the state of the world (all the suffering and conflict). I decided that any harm I may do my soul etc, would be worth the risk knowing that I may be able to help resolve conflict and suffering for possibly thousands if I ended up getting a job with the U.N.

'Oh' I forgot to mention that my life is absolutely curious and 'head shakable' even at the best of times. I was a typical jack the lad until a few months before I joined and spent most of my time from the age of 14 onwards 'messing about' and 'going along' with less desirable extra-curricular activities. Every weekend would see us all (nearly everyone from our estate) trying to get as much cheap booze as possible, then we would spend most of the week being fairly miserable, sitting in our rooms playing computers and getting drunk. We would then wait for the next weekend to 'enjoy ourselves' again (please excuse the 'inverted comas' I have only just found 'em on the keyboard and I want to try and appear 'a slightly literary competence' - if not grammatical - to impress the publishers and me mum).

So I luckily managed to quit that 'less desirable lifestyle' long enough to pass the tests that Army enlistment required. I did incredibly well with someone telling me exactly how to do things and the stability and camaraderie that Army life offered. I had an amazing and highly regarded job (mostly making tea 'Nato' and waiting round for hours, and the usual 'bulling of boots etc' which I will explain more in my Autobiography) I ended up deciding that If I got in a support role then I would stick with it but I totally refused to be an infantry soldier. It was just who I was and how I felt, it doesn't mean I am against being an infantry soldier, on the contrary I am eternally grateful for those very brave men and women who are willing to put themselves in such dangerous positions. I ended up in the corps of royal Engineers. I passed the training (only just as it was very arduous and a lot of heavy lifting, strength and toughness was required as the training was so hard) though I did not feel I would do well and in honesty was quite scared being around such robust and strong lads who worked hard and played very hard. I decided to transfer to the AGC and did some admin work as a clerk serving in N.I and two tours of Afghanistan.

I had a big grand plan....

The way I saw things, ever since I was young, was pretty much like this: Adults were nearly all crazy and the world was severely screwed up. As an adult I have since learnt that I was very much right. The terrifying thing was that nobody seemed to care! The other terrible thing was: that I seemed to care a lot, this was no doubt going to be an 'interesting' life indeed. To add to these ingredients that god created for this life I am living, (he obviously had a 'sense of humour that day') when sending me forth to our beautiful planet; there were also some slight disadvantages he thought he would bestow on me (blight me with…you just wait Mr God!!). I was more or less a still born and for whatever reason this caused me to be severely underweight, half blind and unable to speak. Luckily (or unluckily, as I often feel - as I may not have suffered so much) I was good at persevering. From around the age of three, until I was about seven; I was a young 'Captain Jack Sparrow. in that I wore an eye patch on my 'bad' eye (I had a most severe squint – ok maybe I am glad I 'suffered' (persevered) as I don't think squinty four eyes were too high up on the 'cheerleaders' list of who they should ask to the prom (we don't have proms but disco doesn't sound as good). You have probably guessed that I have just learnt what brackets are for too. Are they called brackets? Anyhoooo....

My family helped me a lot with my speech and I have very fond but vague memories of my brother spending a lot of time saying 'my names not bloomin Dason, its Jason!!' This helped as he was by far the coolest person ever and I was sure he was going to be the next Tom Cruise; so I tried really hard not to offend him and I also tried hard to pronounce his name correctly. This was in between my elder siblings most favourite game of 'lets see if you can beat your best time of getting me a can of juice out of the fridge' a great way of having your very own personal slave (I never did beat my best time – which was obviously my first time; which consequently caused me great frustration and made me want to try harder every time they would ask. The level of their intelligence and enterprise was second to none, God only knows what amazing and wonderful things they would have done with their lives, if they had more opportunity in a 'desirable place'.

My squint got a little better and by the time I reached secondary school and was encumbered with a new found thing called vanity - which we needed to get the girls - I decided to quit with my specs some of the time. This caused quite severe headaches, but my perseverance 'willingness to suffer' eventually paid off, and by the time I was in my mid-teens, I had completely overcome my speech impediment and stopped wearing glasses all together, my squint only showed its ugly head when I was really tired, much to the delight of my 'less sensitive and not so kind' friends. I was still ridiculously skinny and also very small though, around 8 stone and 4' 10 by the time I was 15. Sadly, my life meant I was unable to stretch myself or build myself up very much. I worked hard in factories when I left school, grew a little and got to a healthier – less chance of being bullied – (I've also found these dash things, dunno what there for but what the eck!!) 9 and a ½ stone and around 5'8; plus I had found the ability to stop ************a ****** or 'caring quite so much' as some other more discerning people may put it. I am so glad I grew out of this ability, as so many of my friends that I grew up with, are now dead, in jail or addicted to stuff because they learnt those same 'life skills'.

I survived my childhood and the place that I (not so) fondly call home, a fast developing and up and coming town with some of the best people ever (I actually mean this, they have to be by nature and spirit to want to go there ;-) Corby and Kettering – I was born in Kettering and lived there before I joined the Army - in Northamptonshire.

My ruddy heart would not let me spend my life having fun and enjoying myself in Corby and it was tearing me in two.....

It is terribly hard to leave everyone and everything you know when you have the constitution of a little girl and having hardly ventured out of your hometown, but I did it. I secretly took time away from my friends, family and fun and did weird stuff like read dictionaries and snuck off to the countryside sketching. I got caught several times and received the obligatory 'punishments' from my peers. It was here that I would start to devise my cunning plan to end suffering and all things bad. It was going to be really simple and straight forward and as soon as I quite my beer habit and did a few laps around the block, it was more or less a done deal, all the other humanitarians and peacekeepers may as well hang up their boots. 'Supernerd' was unleashed on the world ;-) Gods sense of humour never fails to amaze me!

Seriously though, my heart would not let me rest and I seemed to feel all the pain and suffering of the world and that around me, through my heart (I felt physically sick most of the time); it was like I was connected to everyone through my heart and I could feel their pain. The only way I could seem to cope without physically trying things, (which I did later – I tried at least) a bit too bloomin much, I may add, due to my feeling that everyone else was shirking in this department (ps let me know if I overdo it with the dashes and brackets, just send a heartfelt and concerned letter to PO box...the one where all the governments concerns go...sure they'll get a fab reply...somewhere near that triangle place where the planes and ships go...) the only way I could cope, was by numbing it with alcohol and other, not particularly healthy or constructive ways (junk food). It was during this time whilst I tried to completely quit being a 'lad' that I went a little mad. I would highly recommend (from my experience anyway, I think you should try different ways to improve your life, health and overall well-being that suits you, as different things work for different people); cutting down gradually depending on the level it effects your mental health. Any habits you try and moderate can have quite severe mental health effects if you try and quit them all in one go. I tried this. After drinking for about 5 years and sometimes quite a lot, I decided to just completely give up. I didn't sleep for nearly 3 nights and started becoming very weird rambling on about 'God is short for good' and 'we are all part of the same energy' etc….(my family must have thought why us?). I think this is when the first fundaments of 'The Penguins theory' really began. If we realised we were all a part of the same thing then maybe we would try and help each other more, make the whole world much more enjoyable and stop so much pain and suffering.

I ran around the block a few times and I quit my habbit and then I……I chickened out of joining. I could feel my families hearts drop ☹. Never fear because a few years later I ran even more laps around the block and moved to a place that was full of positivity and enthusiasm and applied again. This time I was sure to join, I had fully formed my wonderful and great plan: join army, save money and learn why everyone was killing each other; go to Uni and learn other views on why everyone was killing each other and then join the UN. I would then go off and speak to said people, ask them to stop killing each other - as there was much better things to do and enough good things to go around (if there wasn't I would even go back to working in factories to make enough; as it was rather upsetting watching everyone behave like a bunch of ***** or 'people who don't have better things to do or better ways to feel' for those more discerning (discerning means snobs☺, obviously) types.

I had another slight problem though, I was living in a great place, in a beautiful house, with 4 girls who seemed to want to spoil me. Saving the world suddenly seemed much less appealing, but unluckily for me my heart won out and on the morning of 17th September 2001 – 6 days after 9/11 'which sealed my heart and my destiny – I ran down the road with my bin liners and jumped on the train with about 20 seconds to spare and set off for what has been a very curious life indeed.

A few hours later my amazingly brilliant and wonderful Platoon staff seemed to be having a rather bad day and I seemed to be the obvious outlet to their grievances'. I had been up until about 4am having a final farewell leaving party and my fab staff had the notion I had spent the morning preparing for the day at the pub. After a lot of shouting I started crying...(well nearly) and said I wanted to go home, like the little girl I was. They wouldn't let me and after a few weeks I had progressed from a little girl into an old woman. I was feeling much better but Military life was incredibly hard and for some peculiar reason I could not persuade them that the best way to protect our nation was by letting us all sit around playing computers and smoking drinking.

So some of the best Army Instructors in the world soon knocked me into shape. I turned out to be actually quite good at stuff when I pushed, and I had come a long way since my days of being barely able to see or speak. I was the best shot in my platoon (best at shooting guns) I also became one of the fittest and just missed out on 'best improved' recruit (I think they felt I may take this the wrong way ;-) I could not have won best recruit over-all as I was still a lazy git at heart and would never miss an opportunity for a shortcut or two. One of my best shortcuts which I am incredibly proud of to this day as I got away with it was to put my issue t-shirts and trousers straight into my locker from the packet as the packet size was precisely the size they needed to be for inspection in our lockers and they also appeared ironed. Amazingly I left the same one in place and just washed the ones I wore straight away and therefore saved myself many hours of ironing which meant I had much more time for practical jokes, which are a must to get through basic.

After serving a few months in H.M Forces, I quickly realised I would not be made Field Marshal straight away and be able to resolve all the world conflict. So I transferred to a Corps that would mean me possibly being able to hoity toit with them instead (it seemed the next best thing) I got a job being responsible for the admin of British Diplomats and High ranking officers. I feel so honoured looking back. I just wish I wasn't such an insecure introvert whilst I had such great opportunities and experiences, though who can blame me with the start I had in life. I did start to overcome my shortcomings (laziness, fear, intolerance, impatience etc) and I am still working on them too. I am still obviously very unsettled, which Is not the best lifestyle to be able to grow as an individual, but I guess I'm persevering still ;-)

I'd saved up enough money, gained some experience and was all set to go to Uni. I was incredibly looking forward to working with the UN as I held them in such high regard and had been through so much. Mr God, however, was not quite ready for total peace and harmony in the galaxy and decided I should meet a beautiful young lady instead. This was all I ever really wanted for myself; have a family and settle down with someone to share all of life's great stuff with. I decided I could have a relationship and still go to uni and work for the UN or a similar organisation and maybe having a partner would help, as I would have more balance and stability. I felt like I was betraying the world and I soon closed up and turned into a dick long enough to make myself really ill and push her away. To be honest we were not right for each other and things started going wrong with the plans we made from the start. I ended up having to walk away with nothing as I decided I really wanted it to work and 'we would find away'. I ended up a little poorly to say the least and I made a fresh start in Oxford….

My mum and stepdad collected me (my stepdad has since passed away and I very much miss the idea of his presence in my life, he was about the only stable and strong person I had in it and I looked up to him as he was a very decent and kind hearted bloke, or at least that's the way it seemed, as I have since learnt I had lots of great people in my life). I got out the car after pleading, 'turn off here I am going to try Oxford' I got out the car with about £70 odd quid and a few clothes. The next few months were very interesting to say the least...Which I won't delight you with right now, as I am going to save these details for my Autobio. I went to church and asked them if they knew anyone who had a room as the night shelter was not quite the Ritz as I was hoping. I got a room and I then went to another church where they had some wonderful music and singers. I happened to be the only white person their but I did not mind to much as I really like black people and feel quite comfortable around them; perhaps I have the spirit of a black person, though I can't seem to bloomin well dance like them ;-)

I told my new friend Denzel about my misfortune and tales of woe since leaving and how I squandered my chances of going to university with my poor investments and terrible luck and he said I should apply to Oxford Brookes. *We also formed a band together which I christened 'Jabullah and the white man'. Hmmm I thought, yes I'm sure Oxford would love to have me as a student. I applied and he helped with my application (I one day hope to meet him and his wonderful family again and thank him properly, I was so heart warmed at the welcome they gave me and was in admiration of their sense of decency and light-hearted funny mentality they had). The problem was the room I got was with little support or help and was this was too difficult for me to recover. At this stage I was quite severely ill, though I put on a brave face most of the time so probably appeared ok most of the time, hence why I was not given more help from the NHS etc (that'll teach me to pretend to be strong and well – though I was fearful I would be bullied if I appeared weak). I soon went downhill and tried to cope, buy drinking high strength lager to get me through. I quickly became much worse and even more ill, so I decided I needed to try somewhere else. I went off to Cornwall and ended up even more ill than before and I felt so terrible I took a little more paracetamol than one should be prescribed. I woke up on the side of a cliff and was surprised to be alive; 'what on earth are you doing' I thought and decided I must go and stay with family, I felt it had all been for nothing but I knew it would have been a terrible thing to end things properly, even though I was suffering so much. On a lighter note, with fear of depressing you all to death, there was a fantastic warship anchored just off the coast which was rather intriguing. I wondered if they were trying to rescue me, then I just thought Darren you're a moron!! I tried to get home but ran out of money and called me mum; they came and got me and I stayed with them for a few weeks which helped a little. I then went off back to my room in Oxford and decided my only option (I felt I had tried every other possible alternative – from Hospital to working holidays and from Buddhist communities to joining the Army) the only place where I seemed to do well and was reasonably healthy if not content and happy was the Army. The problem was I tried to re-join, as many friends said I should, and they just seemed to mess me around and cause me more frustration (I think they were probably seeing how well I was and that could be said for the NHS and DWP too – or maybe they were just being dicks and did not realise how ill I was or maybe they were just mean – who knows for sure?) at the careers office when I tried to re-join and then re-enquired. I was so heartbroken and sick of this life and especially this country, with everything I had done, gave and put myself through to be left like this and caused so much pain.... the only thing I had not tried and an idea someone put into my head one day was the French Foreign Legion. I had a couple of friends from Afghan who had been in, and from what I heard they were treated well and highly respected. What have I got to lose I thought, I would just do the same as before when I joined our Army and be more careful with who I invested in. This caused me quite some 'inner arguing' with myself.... joining the bloody French!! At heart I am very much an Englishman and I am quite patriotic although I don't always like to show this as I feel the world needs to start to overcome our barriers (such as nationality, culture and language etc) and although today the English and the French are close and dear allies and have a huge amount of appreciation for each other and mostly have the same ethics and standards of living; we have been age old adversaries and going off to join them made me even more pissed at our country for 'forcing me to such absurd measures'. What else could I do though, I would not end things after so much and the thought of my parents and family's feelings, yet my pain and suffering was too much to bare. I booked my ticket on the next morning on the Euro Express and set off.... again I shall not go into too much detail as I'm saving it but here's a little bit of 'my French adventure'*

I arrived in France feeling a little worse for wear after the 10-hour overnight coach trip – don't forget I was very very ill still. I got off the bus and waited around till the tube came which was to take me to the place I believed you could join. Apparently there was some large gates and a tough looking guard standing watch wearing the famous Cape Blanc. I got off the tube and had no idea where I was or where to go…blast my really crud planning. I asked the locals who mostly replied:

'Non Misour' whilst shaking their heads with a very mischievous smile on their faces.

*I got more or less this response and was sent off to a few random places to entertain the locals before I met an elderly gentleman who informed me the ********** was just up the hill and around the corner. Ah well here go's nothing. It was a beautiful sunny day and I had me last fag before I set off up the hill.*

I saw the gates, they looked menacing and unwelcoming. I then saw the guard who looked even more menacing and unwelcoming. I approached with determination and single mindedness, what choice do I have I thought. It really must have seemed like a Mr Been sketch. I approached the gate and enquired:

' Hi I am here to join the legion!'

He looked at me as if I was asking him directions to the zoo, whilst he rolled his eyes....

A month later I failed selection and went home to 'g'ole Blighty'. I was much stronger and healthier although I was still very ill (emotionally ill– I did not realise that this was an actual thing) wait for me book ;-)

I got back to my room and there was a letter for me that stated I had won a place at Oxford Brookes on the foundation year course with a chance of continuing on to the Architects course. I thought wow great as if that's likely. I went back to my room and after a few days of wondering around Oxford (emotionally unwell) I gave my local 'I will numb your emotional wellness shop' a visit and bought just 2 strong lagers. I was now determined to ration my strong lager intake; after another 4 strong lagers later I had a very pleasant sleep although woke up quite sensitive and depressed. I decided to give my rationing a bit of a break as I had been so wonderfully brilliant for the last month (we were not allowed to drink) and I got another few strong lagers. A few weeks later I was still (emotionally unwell) and also now mentally unwell and physically not too great either. I went off again and joined a 'Homeless community' called Emmaus. I tricked myself and by believing I was joining as a volunteer to help the homeless as I did not want to go into the 'Homeless' Bracket; as they don't strike me as the most highly regarded or happiest individuals and after all I was a veteran and had worked my way up to one of the most esteemed jobs there were. I joined Emmaus as a 'companion' which means down and out low life or victim and unfortunate one, depending on one's viewpoint. I didn't really care at least I would not let this life waste the rest of my time here and cause any more illness on my part. I went along to Coventry (apparently that's where you go if you misbehave, a kind gentleman once told me, I thought if that the case it should be bloody full with how I have been treated!!)

I enjoyed it and met some fantastic people. I got stronger and felt mentally and physically much better though yup you guessed it.... that blasted emotional stuff was still loitering with intent. My start date for uni was fast approaching.... (you guessed again, more in me book). I went, I can't begin to explain my time there and would not want to just yet, but, along with other things and especially one very dear and beautiful person and a few other great people it has helped me heal emotionally and probably saved my soul from a long time in a place somewhere far worse. There are three films that have had the greatest effect on my life ***Iron Will****, I cried all night as I was emotionally ill and I think this gave me the determination of 'will' and spirit to want to change my life.* ***The goonies,*** *whats to say, this is how life should be for everyone should it not? ☺and of course* ***'March of the Penguins'*** *we can learn so much from nature and our beautiful world and creatures inspire me all the time – especially those daft and silly Penguins!!*

I had to leave uni early as I could not sustain my illness and after struggling through for five years and not wishing to give up even if it killed me, I became critically ill; I went to stay with family again. I think the defining factor was me quitting eating meat all together, one day I just stopped completely. I became very weak and my ability to crawl along with my illness came to abrupt stop. I recovered and I took some time out as I knew I had pushed myself much too far. I did a lot of walking and I became aware of a feeling that was one of the worst I have ever had. I felt soul-less, I just felt like a shell of a person without any real feeling or persona. I have since realised that when they talk about something being very soul destroying, it was actually true in a literal sense too. I have also learnt that if you keep putting your heart into an aim or goal and continue endlessly without any or little reward or achievement, you can actually lose your soul, or at least that's how it felt. I started walking, that's all I could do really, as I had no money and did not feel up to visiting friends or traveling. I walked on average about 20 miles a day for about six weeks then I became seriously bored and there was risk of me turning to excess again. I managed to get a place in a hostel in London and I thought why not? If I couldn't get work in London and find things to do then I must be a lost cause. It turns out I am a lost cause, I left London, because I started drinking cheap cider and now knowing where that may lead and not wishing to put myself or my family through any more pain I went back to stay with my family again. When I got back however I could feel things had changed in how they felt and they pushed me away, not in a mean way just a little bit of a nudge as if to say; dust yourself down try again and learn from mistakes. I went off and moved to the place I moved to before I joined the Army. I had very little and it was coming up to winter I made myself homeless and was determined to rebuild my life and live somewhere decent. I found a reasonably Ok place to sleep and I joined a hotel gym for somewhere to go and somewhere to shower and stay fit. I loved the staff there they were really kind and had a lot of empathy for my situation. Things were going well and when I got some stability I then sorted out my benefits and told friends of my situation. My friends helped and clubbed together to help and I bought a laptop. It was one night whilst I could not sleep and had been reflecting on my life that I suddenly remembered and found similarities (though hardly quite the same) to those wonderful creatures Emperor Penguins who inspired and heartened me so much in the film 'March of the Penguins'. I then made a sub-consious decision that I was going to walk very far and it was there that I started to write my book 'The penguins theory' which was a theory I had discussed with a friend at Uni. I think he thought I needed to get some emotional illness medication and he bought me some more Ale which helped a lot ☺. I wondered how much better things would be for us if we too could learn to 'put one another first' sometimes as the penguins do through the worst of the winter months when they take turns on the outside (I actually thought if that was us we would all freeze to death, but I do not want to be over cynical to us). I just wondered how the world would be if we had the same sentiment as them in terms of evolving and not just to survive. Who knows? Maybe I would not be laying in a doorstep writing a stupid ruddy book on a Friday morning, I thought!! But I sat there anyway and I typed away and it gave me something to do. I bought a laptop with the help from my friends and I actually started to enjoy and feel a little normal sitting in the hotel bar typing away. I finished the basic main story of part one which was about twenty odd pages and I read it back often which would bring a few tears as I was suffering so much from sleeping rough (my body was in a lot of pain from the floor each night and emotionally it was very hard) and I could relate to much of the frustration and despair of the two Eskimo children and also that of the Penguins. I showed some friends and they said it was really good, but I did not know if they were just saying that or not. Things carried on well and I thought I would even be quite happy settling there and then one week as usual throughout my life as things start to get a little better, disaster strikes.

I left and decided I would try somewhere I had visited a couple of times and felt really warm and decent. I went through all the same stuff until....yup, you guessed it, disaster again....

I left again and I began my walk…'my Penguins Theory walk'. I got on the bus in Cambridge on the 11th of February 2016 and I set off towards Cromer.

As I ventured off for that first morning of the coastal part of my walk, I felt a real sense of purpose; for the first time since I was very young I really felt like I had some control over my life. I had an aim each day and I could do this indefinitely. The days would not be as unbearable as they were staying in one place and I was looking forward to the adventure and even though I did want to turn back my heart quite simply would not let me, if I did I felt like I would be giving up on us, especially those who had invested in me already - my close family and friends and especially those less fortunate.

The coast was beautiful, there was mental stimulation with new scenery, a goal of getting to the next place, something interesting to talk about to the locals (walking 5000 miles, which was my goal at this stage - roughly the distance of the UK coastline) and a bit of fun and excitement too; not to mention the amazing sunrise/sets, stars, nature and the thrill of finding places to sleep each night. Also the exercise would help me get healthier and I would have a healthy place to think. Looking back now; If I planned the journey with campsites and visiting more places of interest, and if my financial position was better, I was a little healthier and had some company now and again, 'it would have been very enjoyable indeed old chap...' ;-)

As I was reaching the top of the hill leaving Cromer, the sun was just rising over the horizon and It felt so good in my soul. I stood for a few minutes watching the sunrise then I marched on with vigour and determination in my heart, there was no stopping me now.....

I took a wrong turn!!! I started to panic. This showed what bad shape I was in and it also showed what a crud map I had. In my naivety, and before I set off I thought that I would be able to manage. 'Nothing to it' I thought. I would just follow the roads that run adjacent to the coast.....and simples!! In my mind anyway! (what a simple and beautiful place it is by the way - mostly.   ;-) I just missed one slight point though; some roads go to the coast and that's as far as they go they just go to the sea, and sadly, do not always veer round along the coast to please dear old center of the universe, moi. This happened on several occasions and it was quite annoying especially if the roads were long. It was about 15 miles in and the souls of my feet were killing, I was so focused on getting to my first destination which was a small village called (need to look at the maps   ;-) which was about 40 miles or so, Including my walking around various places on-route, that I had completely forgot to stop for a breather and food. I pulled over at the side of the road and took off my boots for inspection. I had bought some cheap casual boots from Asda for about 40 quid and they had served me well over the winter months with light walking (15ish miles a day mostly in dry conditions); the only thing now was, they were taking a real pounding and it had been raining a lot lately. The souls had started to disintegrate and my feet new about it. I became more conscious of the pain as I rested and a slow feeling of doubt started to creep in. I felt another wave of panic and made a mental note to save money.

If you ever doing something like wondering around the country, without a clue and your life is hanging in the balance, please don't take mental notes. For important things mental notes are what mental people take. For all that is good and reasonable in the world take real notes and write them on the back of your hand, otherwise you will probably forget. I made a mental note for something important and I forgot to remember it. I suffered about 3000 quid's worth of discomfort as a consequence. My boots reminded me this several days later when one soul totally gave way and dug a sharp grid like pattern into my feet. My highly skilled engineering training - finely honed by 'the best' Army in the world took over (I am so not tough or able, like most the way you would expect most veterans by the way - I'm kind of like a cross between ' The Princess and the pea and Doughal from father ted :-). 'I wonder if any Armies give their recruits a little bit of Intelligent credit and own up to being quite 'a good Army but probably not quite the best', 'Hmm'. I pulled out a library card and put it under the insole of my boot. Ahhh heaven.

The first day flew by in a flash and I had been walking for about 16 hours and was still about 3-4 miles from where I hoped there would be somewhere to sleep. After my night of exuberant drinking (3 beers) I was determined to cut down to a few days a week (of one or two beers) as I wanted to cement the hard work I had put in as I had not drank for nearly a month and I had also cut down smoking (the most disgusting habit ever) and junk food too! I knew that if I cut down to a few beers a week for another month I would be In reasonable control again after nearly a year of very excessive binging on junk food, TV, Alcohol, old sad songs and one of the worst things in this day and age (for those who have crud lives 'nostalgia'!) from stress and sleep deprivation.

As I was walking down the road towards my first place to stay the sky was so beautiful; and as I used to when I was young, I reflected on myself, us, and our world from the perspective of everything around us 'Our home, the Milky Way'.

It was a clear night. In the winter, the moon, stars and planets shine that much brighter. I spent most of the late evening looking up and appreciating how tiny we were in the vastness of space. It made me feel quite petty and shallow, letting my emotions and feelings overwhelm me, when they are just a tiny tiny part of us. I suppose we forget this with the modern world and all the pressures and stress we are put (and put ourselves) under. Most of the time (although we know our individual life is a tiny part of everything) 'most of the time' the way we feel as individuals, is everything! and we often lose our sense of being part of and connected to each other and nature.

I watched a shooting star fly past and made my usual wish, that I don't have to say as I know it off by heart as does God. It's not for world peace or an audi R8 as you may think; (maybe a little bit this :-). As I don't think we are ready for total peace yet (everything) and I don't think it would get the best from us if there was, absolutely straight away (a little faster perhaps especially ending poverty, but most things need to grow reasonably and naturally - especially us, with free will and inspiration and not by complete and total force - though that's just me....who knows for sure?). I feel we have to grow, and evolve first (with fun, and joy, health, education and culture and of course kindness and recycling) I do wish however, that we can one day have more of these things and the means to enjoy them and overcome our shortcomings. I pray we can make our home and lives as wonderful and beautiful as they can be.

I walked on and I started to heal........ 'emotionally heal'.

After a week or so into the walk I started to have feelings that I had not felt since I was a young child of around 8-9. It was those wonderful feelings of excitement, joy and wonder and at the same time feeling safe. Of course, I was very far from being safe in the literal sense. Though over the last year or so I had learnt that even if things are terrible for us and we feel alone and vulnerable, if we can learn to open our hearts to everything then it will protect us (I think this is what real faith is – its not just about Leaders, Nations or religions-its about having faith in everything) as my following poems describes:

Sword and shield

What is my heart for, they ask to me.
Alas, it is my sword and my shield,
I say, the love I feel can shield me from pain,
And the joy and kindness, can, likewise cut through darkness.

It is our essence and being and connection to each other and God;
Though it is long buried, deep, under layers of hardships, that we've endured whilst making this harsh and cruel world our home.

But fear no longer my good friends, for we have appeased Mother Nature in this place of wonder and she is starting to share her beauty and offer her jewels.
But we must respect her, I beseech you this, for she can suddenly turn; and the comforts and joy we have earned can so easily be taken, if she wishes; we can be thrown into the abyss of space and time in a much poorer state than when we arrived and this hell can last such a great length of time.

So let us worship and praise her and look after her so, as she looks after us all; for she is our home and whilst we are here she is in our hearts. So with our shield lets protect her and let's cast more light upon her with our sword.

Let us rejoice with her, for we still have some heart and spirit and she shall return much more than we gave, as long as we have faith in her and respect her.

Over the next few months I started to undo some of my many years of armour that I had layered up to prevent any more pain. I also thought about a lot of things, mostly how we all got in such a mess and how much better it could be **'when we are ready'** I feel that this point is hugely important to global development. We could make and build the best and most wonderful place that anyone could ever imagine but if we ourselves are not healthy, content and joyful; then it won't matter too much how the world is. I really think we have as much work to do on ourselves as we have on our home until things improve considerably, but for this to happen we must make more facilities (both literal and whatever the opposite from literal is.

I have experienced a lot of different things from a lot of different perspectives and I hope one day to be able to write about this, when I am in a healthier and more relaxed environment to write, as I realise that writing about things that matter can do harm if you're not feeling great yourself and in the right place. I'm in a public library with some wonderful elderly ladies having a good old natter about cancer and stress and lots of other fab stuff ☺ bless em. I do hope I can find such a place, one day perhaps.

Darren Greg Johnson 14/11/16

During my walk around the coast I was so inspired and heartened by nature. Every day would reward me with something fun or beautiful, whether it was ducks pranking about and laughing at us (as they often do) or an awe-

inspiring sunset. It was during this time that I felt my desire to paint landscapes increase significantly. The seasons were changing from Winter (which is not the most fun time to be sleeping rough) to spring and this is no doubt the most incredible transition that nature go's through. You really feel new life start to form and the joy of seeing lambs running around and trees start to blossom and birds start to sing loudler, really is what its all about. Its these experiences that are so special, the only thing I wished at the time was that I could have shared them with a loved one, as sadly these times are few and far between for me ☹ I have had a few though and I am grateful for them, its those feelings that we take with us and that is all that is really worth saving whilst we're here. That and a few quid for a rainy day obviously ☺

Being outside constantly, from winter to spring, really is a soul enhancing experience and I would really recommend it to everyone. Staying on campsites obviously, as sleeping rough causes you to be a bit hard stressed and unable to fully appreciate the joy of it. I had a lot of time to reflect on all aspects of life and as I have experienced many things from many perspectives I really hope the clever clog nerds can make some use of me walk.

My aim was to walk around 5,000 miles to get well and raise money and inspire others to live fuller lives. Since I set off on that cold February morning I have walked somewhere in the region of 10,000 miles and I am planning to continue my journey on cycle and complete 24,000 (hopefully with a little more comfort.

The Penguins Theory really grew from those feelings of pain, heartache and fear that seemed so overwhelming as a kid. It was a mixture of my early years, feeling the pain and sorrow of so many people and then the inspiration of my family (especially my Mum and later eldest Brother) that really sowed the PT seeds. These emotions mixed with (what was one of my escapisms) Movies provided me with the bitter-sweet passion needed to drive me to go to the extremes I have. I have suffered a lot of pain and long periods of suffering trying to improve things and sometimes I am not sure what the eck is wrong with me. In truth, I am an able person and have so much going for me. I am a talented artist and have a wealth of experience and friends which would give me the means to live a fulfilling and peaceful life and probably even happy too. The thing is my heart simply would not let me; I can't fully explain the feeling but I would compare it to having the most amazing girlfriend, family, job and most loyal and wonderful family pet and learning that you would lose them all tomorrow. This is similar to how my heart feels most days and I feel if I don't try I would lose them all....maybe there is even some truth in this, if you think more profoundly in the future for us all.

I am very happy to announce though, especially to my family and friends that this feeling has subsided considerably since last year and now my heart is nearly fully focused on improving my own life and that of close friends and family.

So that is how 'TPT' came about....but what exactly is the theory?

Well the theory is the most simple and obvious thing in the world; unless you have not thought about it that is.

Please excuse the 'Darrens version of history and logic lesson' but I really feel it is important to appreciate how we have evolved and, thus, how the less wonderful things have grown; only then can we properly begin to be able to improve things and most importantly 'make up' (to ourselves and our world) for the harm we have been afflicted to and part of, ***from the hardships that this earth has caused****. This understanding helped me to find forgiveness and was probably the most important thing I learnt I am sure this grew from brookes so I am* *very grateful to that academic institution for that.*

I am very sure of this much: (please excuse the lack of technical jargon and proper terminology, I am sorry if this offends you if you're a bit of a boffin, nerdy type of person)

We are all an organic physical body (that has evolved from other bodies since our time here). We all have a conscious energy within our body (this is how we know who we are and not someone else) that is unique to us. This energy is most probably a part of (albeit partly and temporarily detached from each other whilst in our bodies) a larger entity (often refered to as our spirit) that becomes more or less positive depending on the things we experience and the choices we make with our minds and our hearts. We evolved from apes and became able to do amazing stuff. We took control and ownership (by way of the effects we have on it) of our planet and all the other living creatures in it. All life here on earth is depending on us to make a path to heaven or hell (our over-all spirit becoming more or less positive and feeling good). As our numbers increased from our earliest ancestors we had to explore new places in search of food and resources. This caused us to grow apart as a tribe and to also become murderers as we needed to survive and we most probably followed the influence of other predators at the time and one day one person decided to kill another creature. Later on we met up again with our long lost family but did not recognise them very well as they were being a bit weird and had 'changed'. They were obviously evil, so we killed em and used there amazing stuff!! Yay! We started to grow to enjoy and depend on these feelings of war and conflict and it made us feel all heroic and 'manly'. We learnt and built new amazing stuff and ventured even further. Much later we met even more weird people and won even more amazing stuff!! Wooohooo. We started to evolve and develop into human beings. We found civilised ways to live. We learnt a lot, we realised they were not weird, we realised that we had won a little of what did not really matter and lost nearly everything that did.

Hooorah that's my history of everything. We are learning how to 'make up' for things this earth caused us, that we were afflicted to and through little choice, did. One of the ways that I try to make up for my shortcomings is to firstly simply try and look after myself and be healthy. Over the last two years I have done quite well and managed to cut down considerably the amount I smoke, drink and procrastinate. I read more, keep active, socialise more and do a lot more constructive stuff. Over the last few months I have even managed to quit smoking completely, quit social drinking (as my life's too stressful and I don't wish to take the risk as its easy to get carried away). Which I am very proud of, although my biggest sense of achievement is quitting eating non-free range chicken (sadly I have quit eating em altogether as I can't find any free range cooked and I don't have a portable oven to squeeze in me bag – this saddens me greatly as I miss Nandos more *than anything). I have also quit eating lamb and don't eat much fish either. I have also cut down my beef intake and pork (this is what I eat mostly) I figured lambs are too cute and they give us wool and milk and they don't carry a huge amount of meet per one life. Whilst Pigs and Cows carry a huge amount of meet, so its less murdering, until our bodies evolve to sustain meat free; maybe in a few millennia or so (I have a 20 year plan to cut down to an kilo a month). Sadly, the amount of junk food has stayed the same but I'm not too fussed as I have been walking an average of 20 miles a day. I don't miss the food that much and I actually am starting to feel the benefits of the healthier diet now things are a tiny bit more comfortable (I have a couple of sponges out of some chairs to sleep on - they are light to carry and comfy). I have also quit weight lifting, this has made me feel a little worse, though whilst on the streets it's not good to feel to healthy as it makes you that much more conscious to how s**t things really are.*

So there it is, that's a little rough guide to Johno's absurd and 'head-shakeable' life. That is how 'The Penguins Theory' grew and what it is and that is also a little intro to the next part of this book which is a shortened version of the main novel, as I explained at the start of my drivel… ☺ 'toodaloo' and I very much hope you enjoy it and feel free to leave great reviews.

Here are a few photo's from my Army life and my walk etc. Thank you very kindly and I hope you have a wonderful and fulfilling life, if you don't I hope you go for a wander…..

I'd had enough of sitting around feeling sorry for myself. I won't ever get a chance to live this life at this time again I thought. Plus I couldn't find a razor in Cambridge!!

One of the sunsets from my walk which was pictured in St Ives, cornwall.

All that rubbish about how wonderful I am as I'm quitting so much meat...hmm.

This was actually one of my favourite moments, cooking wild steak and I felt all wild and adventurous. I nearly set fire to my stuff though, I think the cows spirit made it a bit windier that day ☺

The bus stop which I camped in for a night, not the comfiest of stays though an improvement from the church doorway in a graveyard in the middle of nowhere, so creepy dudes!!! Sorry about the crud images, I sold my good phone for my new adventure.

This is my favourite snap, just to think I lugged this around the coast for nearly a month, since I have had worse things to carry. I have had some peculiar looks to say the least as if to say ' what on earth are they making that poor man do now' why can't they just let him paint his wonderful paintings and marry Jess form 'who's that girl".

I didn't see this, but it's all around us.

Me and the boss (a fantastic and down to earth, kind and amazing woman- well I would say that!!), I really hoped, if things kicked off, she could fight ☺

I have to admit, I never really liked lunching out with the locals, the goats heads were always a stomach turner, but I was big and strong and could eat anything...raaaaaa!!

Swimming in the Panshir Valley which I believe this river ran down from the 'Everest Mountains' (forgot the name of the mountain range ☺.

Myself looking rather awesome and a dear friend and all-round great bloke. 'Gramps'.

In the background there is a 'Hercules' transport plane which we would drive our armoured 4x4s onto and then swan off to some other beautiful part of the country. If it was our day to drive we would have to make sure that we did not fill the wagons up completely as it put the planes over the required payload to take off. I forgot and had to spend a night trying to syphon all the diesel from the engine, my mate got a mouthful, Thank you Pete ☺

Anyone order a Humvee??? You knew when the Americans were around as they never travelled light. This was good sometimes but put a lot of the local's backs, I was glad to know they were there though.

In a black hawk with the Yanks. I really like Americans (Generally), which I think grows from E.T and The Goonies mostly☺. I loved flying in the Blackhawks though on one occasion the boss told the Pilot to show Cpl (never did quite make F.M) Johnson what it could do. The thing dropped out of the sky and I reminded everyone how the French speak ☺ Thanks Boss!!

Using my peripheral vision and relying on my highly trained ninja skills....'Hi mum what ya having for dinner again?' ;-)

This was sometimes the safest way to communicate as the radios were vulnerable.

Feeding a Blue Tit in Hyde park (near the Peter Pan statue), so humbling and wonderful. Love the little pterodactyls, haven't they grown so sweet!!!! It really is a gift and the trust we have built up is great, I hope many of you can go and do this.

What it's all about really.... the family we lost....found again...left behind....and are now beginning to open our hearts too. It's been a long time, I hope they don't feel too badly towards us, though who would blame them if they did. I hope I can take some books next time instead of just pens and pencils.

Me doing amazing adventurous stuff...nah this is in fact a real life adventurer and not just a homeless bum, with little better to do than wander round the country.

I'm sure you can guess where my inspiration for my 'best' oil paintings the world has ever...yeah ok!!

You'd be surprised what a little wander, shave and shower can do. All you need is love…and fresh air helps too.

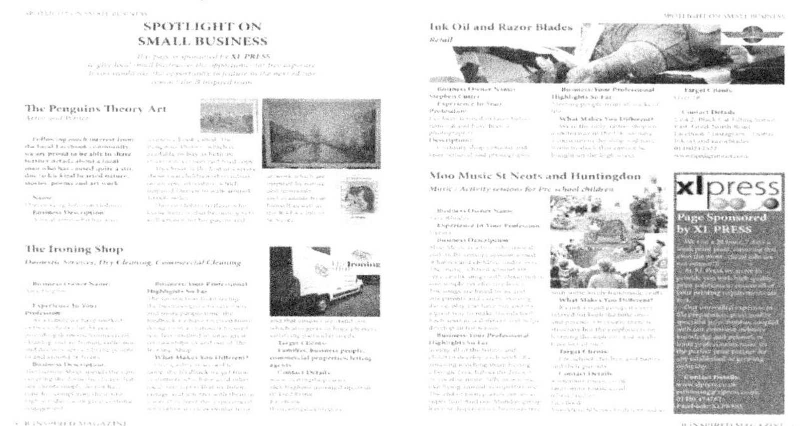

SPOTLIGHT ON SMALL BUSINESS

The Penguins Theory Art

The Ironing Shop

Domestic Services, Dry Cleaning, Commercial Cleaning

Business Owner Name

Experience In Your Profession

Business Description

Business/Your Professional Highlights So Far

What Makes You Different?

Target Clients

Families, business people, commercial properties, letting agents

Contact Details

Ink Oil and Razor Blades

Retail

Business Owner Name

Stephen Cutter

Experience In Your Profession

Description

Business/Your Professional Highlights So Far

What Makes You Different?

Target Clients

Contact Details

Moo Music St Neots and Huntingdon

Music / Activity sessions for Pre school children

Business Owner Name

Experience In Your Profession

Business Description

What Makes You Different?

Business/Your Professional Highlights So Far

Target Clients

Contact Details

xlpress

Page Sponsored by XL PRESS

Contact Details

On my way to super stardom and a super bank balance too ☺ Ok at least I can humour them.

Practising my trade at a difficult time. Notice the lack of specs? bring on the ladies!! You'd think butter wouldn't melt!! This was a difficult time for us, the eighties really set us back a while.

The Waltons….my most beautiful and 'put up with anything' 'why us' Siblings.

My favourite wee neice and nephew…until I find a pic of my other fav wee neice and nephew ☺

My favourite wee neice and her Dad my ex-brother in law. I was hoping she was going to provide 'an old granny' photo like she really is but she insisted on a diva one ☺

Ferris Bewler obviously. Less said the better…I was learning how to be cool and popular arghhhhh!! You twat!!

Part 1

For my brother (s)...

According to ancient Elder belief, it was once thought that all living creatures and human beings were spiritually connected through their hearts. It was said that when we used to live our lives virtuously, *'before we became predators that is'*, that we could feel all of 'the holy spirit' in our hearts and each other's pain and joy. Sadly, as the harshness of this planet drove us to greater extremes, including fighting and killing for survival; meant that over time, we lost this ability and grew into hard hearted and cold blooded killers. It was also believed that if one day we could appease Mother Nature, she would reward us with a planet of plenty and more wonderful and beautiful things than we could imagine. It would then be up to us to see if we were worthy of such a great existence for what could be a long, long time indeed. But first we would have to overcome the monsters that we had become, the only way this was possible was something known 'similarly' to an ancient Latin term known a 'redivivus', which meant to recycle a negative into a positive. There was also an ancient prophecy that told of 'An event of great consequence' that would happen during a 'Show from the Gods'.

This is a story about that event, the event that changed the future of all mankind and Gods creatures; this is how it all began……

Lylamei lived in a small Eskimo village in the Antarctic, along with her parents Geomei and Orloff. Their village had a warm glow, from the many different coloured lights, that would hang from people's doorways and from the nearby trees. The lights would glisten from the icicles that hung from the roof tops and from telegraph posts. There was a warm and positive feeling and a great sense of community and fun, which was shared by all the 200 or so residents. The Aurora or 'Northern Lights' as they were commonly known by westerners danced constantly overhead on the clear evenings and resembled the fluidity of a beautiful ballet.

'They are the dance of the Gods' Lyla was often told by orloff.

Their life was simple and mostly happy and peaceful; they would fish during the mornings and sometimes visit other neighbouring villages on their sled, which was pulled by their Huskies Yakout, Moomin, Arkambacher, Nicholas and Akash.

Their huskies loved pulling their sled which seemed strange to Lylamei as it appeared to be like such hard work. Lylamei was quite young at 6 years of age but she was already able to fish, cook and sew; and she was wise beyond her years thanks to her father and also the village Elder, though she still did not quite

understand why the Huskies loved such hard and strenuous work. Her father Orlof had tried to explain to her that for centuries Huskies had been used to pulling sleds to carry things and because of their 'evolutionary nature' - which they got passed down from their ancestors and their 'spirit' family' in heaven - they needed to be active and working, as that's what they were used too and what made them happy.
Although Lylamei was very bright, she did not quite know how living things could get their body types and their nature from things that were no longer alive. Orlof would merely say that there's more to life than the living things here on earth Lylamei, which just frustrated Lylamei as she thought he was a little bit senile and had spent too long star gazing and watching the Aurora. He would sometimes stay out for hours just staring up into space.

'this was obviously not good for his sanity' thought Lylamei.

It was approaching winter, the nights were getting darker; and the temperature was getting colder than they could remember. On one particular clear night during the Draconids meteor shower - which Lylamei loved to watch - they lay together staring up into space.

"Where does space end Dad?" asked Lylamei.

"Space goes on forever, my dear Lylamei. Did you think there was a brick wall with a sign saying this is the end of space?"

"No, but how can it go on forever it doesn't make sense, everything has to have an end."

This thought made Lylamei feel a little dizzy thinking about it and a little bit queasy too.

"Some things, we are not supposed to understand or figure out my dear, some things we are just meant to enjoy" said Orlof, before adding

“If we figured everything out, then we would know as much as God and Mother Nature and would lose our sense of humanity and not enjoy things so much; everything would lose its magic and wonder ".

Lylamei let the words sink in before asking:

“so why are the scientists and philosophers trying so hard to figure everything out then?"

Orlof replied with a look on his face that showed he was expecting such a question from his bright and beautiful daughter

“It was important to learn some things to try and make life easier and more enjoyable for everyone and to help shape a better world. Though some people take things too far and delve beyond reason and moderation. Some people want to play God and keep pushing boundaries of science further and further". For the sake of us all I hope that they don't open Pandora's Box and if they do I hope they can find their way back, so that science can be used for good and not to play God".

Lylamei thought she knew what Orlof was harping on about but just as she tried to comprehend it, she saw the first meteor shooting across the night sky with its tail blazing behind it.

Letting Orlofs words sink in, she then started to perceive just how tiny she was when she began to look beyond the world around her and look up. She had been reading about space and astronomy in a book she got from a neighbouring village, where, once a month, they got a container of supplies and materials from the closest modern town which was over a thousand miles away. She had learnt that we all lived on a place called earth, which was quite huge and amazing in its own right, with its diverse life forms and different landscapes. She knew there are about 8 billion people on earth and also around

20,000,121,091,000,000,000 (give or take a few trillion here or there) living creatures with feelings and intelligence, which humans were responsible for. This thought made Lylamei very frightened as she knew that she herself was responsible for a few hundred billion lives (wow what a lot of lives, she pondered); real conscious living creatures that God and Mother Nature had entrusted her with.

This made the petty squabbles in her village seem stupid and made her own worries and problems seem selfish and immature. Yet sometimes, it was like her life was all that mattered because her feelings and emotions were so strong. She hoped she would remember this the next time she got upset and things didn't go quite right for her, after all she was responsible for all those lives, she had no time to worry about herself any longer. At that moment, just after she saw her first meteor and thought of all the creatures and people depending on her, she made a promise to try her very best to look after them all, as best as she could. She would start off with the Penguins, as they seemed to have very harsh lives and a lot of them were dying because of the terrible winters they had recently.

After several hours of laying under the stars watching the meteor shower, along with other Eskimos from their village, Orlof picked up Lylamei and put her on his shoulders for the short journey back to their igloo. Geomei had prepared a fish stew for supper and they all huddled together and enjoyed their meal whilst reflecting on their day. After supper Lylamei kissed her parent's good night and went off to bed where she lay thinking of her new responsibilities and if she could be strong enough to manage them; after all, she was only a girl and not even very strong when compared with other Eskimo children, especially Malakei who was the strongest boy in the village and always pushing Lylamei about in front of the other children because they laughed when he made fun of the weaker children. One thing for sure was that if Lylamei was going to be able to look after so many of God's creatures, she would need to get a lot stronger; though, as Geomei pointed out to her time and again, 'physical strength does not compare to having a good spirit on your side'. Geomei told her that physical strength and force rarely does any good in the long term and that goodness, happiness and prosperity are only achieved through hard work, selflessness and inspiration. Lylamei did not agree with this, as Malakei always seemed happy and having fun, and he was always getting what he wanted by force. Geomei would often say that although he may seem happy on the outside, by treating other people in such a bad way, he was causing his spirit a lot of pain, which would one day be to much for him to take and he would no longer be happy and seem to be having fun, but instead he would feel sad and empty. Geomei also added that even if he was lucky enough not to feel bad in this life he would suffer in his next for sure unless he can make up for the pain he has caused. Lylamei knew it was very difficult to make up for hurting people and that if you didn't your soul would have a horrible time waiting in space until it's next body was ready for it on earth.

Kaliffa, the village elder, had once told everyone "for every drop of pain you cause someone, a cup of joy was needed to make up for it, and if not, a bucket of pain you would suffer in your next life".

"It was basic physics" Orlof told her.

Orlof new all about these things from his time in the 'Learned Mountains of Hemlay' where the spirits would sometimes put on displays of colours for the 'living people' to watch. Orlof had been taught that by harming another living creature you caused your soul to become very negative and eventually you would feel this negative feeling *'also known as evil'* when you go to your next body.

Lylamei did not know if all this stuff was true though it did seem logical and it also felt right in her heart. She knew everyone had a spirit inside their body; she had managed to work this much out herself. She thought there must be something different with everyone apart from having a body and a mind, otherwise you would not know that you are you. There must be a conscious spirit inside your body that lets you know it's looking out your eye’s otherwise you would not know which body and mind is you. This made a lot of sense the more she thought of it and so did reincarnation, as she knew we have been born once into a body on earth so there’s a good chance our spirit will be born into a different body (probably depending on how negative it feels or how much good or evil it has done) in the future until the end of this world.

"I guess that's like heaven and hell" she said to the village elder.

Kalifa replied "we are in heaven my dear we just had to go through hell to get here, but we sure don't need to go back there, we must learn from Gods creatures and if we do not, then we shall spend an eternity in hell whilst there is life on earth".

This seemed such a stupid thing to say and Lylamei thought he should probably be sacked as village elder and the job be given to Orlof who explained things much better.

“why should we learn from animals if we are their masters? " asked Lylamei to Kalifa

Though she did not get a reply, as he was now in some kind of trance and mumbling a load of gobbledygook. At least that's what Lylamei thought anyway. He was actually praying to God for the wisdom spirit to share some light with Lylamei and help her on the amazing journey she was soon to take.

With all these things racing through Lylamei's mind she lay in bed for hours trying to get to sleep as she was very worried she would not be able to cope with everything she had learned and she really did not want to spend the rest of her time on earth in a state of hell as Kallifa told her could happen. She then realised that although worrying was sometimes good, too much was very bad and instead she should go out and do things to try and help make things better, firstly for the penguins and then hopefully for all the other creatures she now realised she was responsible for. Maybe then she would even be able to help stop all the fighting between the neighbouring villages as she was dreadfully fearful of all the pain that had been caused to her friends and family over the last few years.

Lylamei said a prayer to the Eskimo god of courage, who's name she had forgotten but rhymed with Kirk or something like that. She prayed for the Penguins who were freezing to death and also the villagers who were all hurting each other because of greed and jealousy. She then thought back to the beautiful meteor shower she had seen and drifted off to a peaceful and long sleep.

The next day Lylamei clambered out of her bed and quickly got dressed in her favourite 'super duper' fur coat and trousers and grabbed her rucksack for her day's adventure to try and save the penguins. Lylamei walked to her best friend's igloo which was only a few igloos down and in the same direction where the Penguins lived. Her best friend was a boy called Pallamo and was two years older than Lylamei but Lylamei thought she was much smarter than Pallamo as he could not even sew yet (she did not realise that boys did not like sewing as it made them seem like big sissies and would mean that they might get bullied from Malakei and his bunch of goons. But he never actually said this, as boys were not allowed to tell girls how they really felt as this was deemed very uncool by all the boys, from all the villages.

Pallamo's parents were often fighting as they had lost everything they owned when the last raid on their village took place a few months ago. This was why Lylamei chose Pallamo as her best friend as she knew he needed her to help him keep his spirits up and to be there for him when his parents were arguing. This happened quite often so it meant Pallamo spent much of his time wandering around the village on his own or out with Lylamei watching the penguins and copying their daft walks and belly sliding that they did.

Pallamo's mother, Arilia, answered the door, she was very beautiful and all the men from the village would secretly hope she would split with her husband so she could be with them; but even though they argued a lot they were in love with each other so much and one day would be able to find happiness when their village wars stopped and they could rebuild their lives and home again as beautiful as they once were.

“Good morning Lylamei” Greeted Arilia as she answered the door.

“Good morning” replied Lylamei.

Lylamei hoped she would one day be as beautiful as Arilia when she was older so that one of the boys would want to marry her and look after her as although she was very good at most things, she could not hunt or build igloos as the work was too hard and only the men of the village could do these things.

“Is Palamo ready to come and play?” asked Lylamei, in a slightly rushed manner.

“yes he is, he is just getting his bag and coat.”

“Ah, thank you very much”

Palamo came out the front door with his bag which he took everywhere 'in case of emergencies' he had told Lylamei. He was very good when it came to emergencies and had once rescued a baby from the village, who was nearly eaten by a Polar Bear. Lylamei did not know if this was true or not, but Pallamo had a lot of stuff in his bag including some rope, a knife, compass, torch and even some bandages; so it was reasonable to believe he fought off a polar bear with all his stuff he that he took everywhere. Pallamo tried to always be tough when he was with Lylamei and thought of her as his little sister more than his best friend which Lylamei quite liked as it made her feel safe. Though he was quite strong and had a bag of things to help with emergencies like Polar Bear attacks; she worried about him very much as he had become much quieter since the other village ruined his last home and stole all his family's belongings. Having parents who argued all the time must be very hard thought Lylamei, whose mother and father had always treated each other well and never argued at all except sometimes when Orlof would spoil Lylamei too much.

“Pallamo, I have something very important to tell you but you must promise not to tell anyone, as it’s a special quest I have been given from our ‘Spirit Family’ in heaven.”

Pallamo thought Lylamei had gone a little crazy from eating too many ‘ice sugar cones’ but Lylamei told him she had not had anything to eat all morning so he listened to Lylameis’ story about her visit with the Village Elder and her meeting with the ‘Spirit Family’ during the night.

Palamo said to Lyla “so what your saying is we have to find a way to save all the penguins which are freezing to death, then help a few trillion other creatures and to top it all, save our villages from war with each other?”

“Pretty Much” was Lyla’s short reply, although she herself had not yet worked out how she could do this or even if it could be done. But their ‘spirit family’ asked her so she had to try at least, the thought of eternal hell on earth helped make it an easy choice, as she didn’t like the idea of this.

As they walked to where the penguins spent their days, Lyla came up with an idea that would surely help the penguins to stop freezing to death. She was very good at sewing and reasoned that if she found a bunch of old fur skins and animal hides she could sew them into penguin coats; just like Mrs Bloomolei had made for their Huskies. They would only have to catch them and one at a time could tie the coats around them so it wouldn’t fall off. The penguins would then be a lot warmer in their new coats and Lyla could then concentrate on helping all the other creatures she was responsible for. So they set off on their quest together, two young souls on a journey that would test their friendship their courage and even their very own life spirits.

As they started on their journey towards the local penguin hangout, which was a little area where the ice had broken on the surface and they could go swimming and belly sliding, Pallamo reasoned that if what Lyla had told him was true, then he too was responsible for lots and lots of living creatures. This had the opposite effect on Pallamo as it did on Lyla and he was very excited at the challenge that lay ahead; plus it would help him forget about his life at home which was full of anguish and heartache, though hopefully that would change soon. He also thought that because he was a boy and two years older than Lyla then he was responsible for more lives than Lyla was and so this naturally made him the leader and meant he was in charge.

Pallamo said to Lyla that "as I am the leader I think it's important we make a plan and the first thing on our plan is where to find the fur we need to make the coats?"

Lyla thought that although Pallamo was older than she was and also had a bag of stuff they might need, she was obviously, by far, much more clever than Pallamo, so although she agreed to let him be the leader secretly she knew she was the leader but would just let Pallamo think he was, for the sake of his boyish pride and ego.

"Well Pallamo, as you're the leader what do you think we should do to try and find some fur?"

"ah I know" Replied Pallamo, with a twinkle of hope shining from his eyes

"we can go and hunt some seals and sea lions and make some penguin coats from them"

Pallamo had obviously not thought this through very well and Lyla immediately saw the dangers of hunting big sea lions with their big dangerous tusks and seals with their huge strong tails. So with a little bit of tact (which basically meant using your brain to think things through properly and also a little bit of clever thinking) she suggested a better way of getting fur to make the coats.

“do you know of anywhere where there are sometimes old bits of fur laying around the place?” Lyla asked Pallamo.

Pallamo started to wonder if such a place existed then he started to think about where there could possibly be some old fur that nobody wanted.

“ I know!” stated Pallamo

“Mrs Bloomolei, sometimes throws out old bits of fur into her bins behind her clothes store down at fox lane”

“Wow, what a fantastic idea Pallamo. You really are the best leader ever” Lyla replied and then gave him a huge hug and a kiss on the cheek.

Pallamo blushed a little and then felt a wonderful sensation in his heart which gave him a new lease of energy from the ‘spirit family’. This was great for Pallamo and suddenly became very excited about their new adventure together and made him feel that there was something worth living for and there was some goodness and hope left in this world. Pallamo felt very lucky to have Lyla as his friend and realised how terrible his life would be without her and their adventures together. Little did young Palamo know that Lyla was equally lucky to have him as her friend and that sometime in the near future he would actually save her life and help her overcome her monsters that would try and stop her from fulfilling her dreams of helping to bring peace to her family, her village and also her heart.

They set off towards Mrs Bloomolei's clothes shop which was on the way to penguin cove and they didn't look back.........

The son had risen in the sky and the early morning clouds were a beautiful pink colour, the seagulls were screeching overhead and there was joy in their hearts. It took them a while to reach the shop which was really just a big tepee, like the Indians used in the wild west of America. They went inside where Mrs Bloomolei was busy at work, creating all kinds of amazing garments from more furs than they had both ever seen.

Lyla greeted the shop keeper in her normal friendly way "Good morning Mrs Bloomolei".

" good morning kids what are you two doing here so early? "

"We are trying to find some old bits of material so we can learn to make some clothes as beautiful as yours.". Lyla replied.

" ah, very well kids then you will need some of my 'cut offs' that I don't need any more and will you be needing a needle too kids? "

Palamo searched through his bag but could not find a needle, which he thought 'I must try and get a needle and some thread or I will never be able to help Lyla on her quest' so he wrote it in his special diary his Dad had given him for Christmas.

After searching his bag Palamo replied that "yes please if you have one we could use, that would be great".

Mrs Bloomoleis tepee was huge inside, much bigger than it looked from the outside. *'Mrs Bloomolei must be some kind of magician or something'* thought Lylamei.

Not only did she have lots and lots of fur and other material but towards the back of the shop were a lot of starnge looking contaptions that were mostly made of brass or something and there were also lots and lots of draws that had hundreds and hundreds of nuts and bolts and screws and things. As well as a big workbench there was a huge light, a bit like the one in the dentist in the 'modern town'. *'I bet that is Mr Bloomoleis' Lyla assumed*

" I do have one, and in fact you can keep it for your special quest and you can also have some old furs that I am not going to use " and with that gave Lyla a wink.

This made Lyla a little surprised, did Mrs Bloomolei Know about her special quest from the 'spirit family' and if so how? And if she knew did any of the other grown-ups know? And if they all knew then why couldn't they all help? Lyla was very perplexed indeed but she did not let it get the better of her. Whatever everyone else knew or no matter what anybody else did or didn't do did not change what she had to do and her responsibility. As long as she did her part and maybe a little more for the ones who were not able to, then Lyla could find peace at least in her own heart, if not in her life. They thanked Mrs Bloomolei for everything and left her to her work whilst they prepared for their journey ahead.

It did not take them long to reach Penguin Cove, but nothing could have prepared them for what they saw when they arrived. There were literally hundreds of dead penguins spread around the cove and there were probably over a few thousand left walking around trying to keep warm. They could see that some of the weaker penguins were starting to tire from fatigue, with all the walking they were doing. Lyla was horrified and heartbroken, she had never seen such a terrible sight even when the neighbouring village would pillage and steal from their own, there was never anyone really hurt or any deaths. This kind of pain and suffering, Lyla had never felt and her heart could no longer bare the emotion any longer and tears began to streak down her cheeks. Pallamo was equally shocked at the sight and although he had been witness to some awful arguing and sadness within his own home, the tragedy that lay before him saddened him and also angered him. Lyla had never seen Pallamo angry before as he was usually too sad and withdrawn with problems at home after they had lost all their belongings. She even felt a little afraid at the level of his fury, which snapped her out of her own despair as she tried to calm him down.

“please calm down Palamo, getting angry will not help them or us” Lyla pleaded with Pallamo, though her words had little effect on his rage.

“How can God and Mother nature be so cruel why would they not bring out the sunshine so the penguins do not have to suffer!!” He bellowed, as loud as thunder itself.

Lyla tried again to get Pallamo to calm down though he seemed to get more angry with every dead penguin he laid his eyes on.

“They do not really care” he fumed.

“If they did they would stop the wind from howling, Jack frost from frosting and make the sun shine brighter!!” and with that outburst he started kicking the snow in such a rage Pallamo seemed like a wild beast, who had been trying to protect its young but was greatly wounded. His hurt was overwhelming his sense of control and his sense of goodness was so offended that he lashed out at the snow and ice rocks. Lyla could see that if he did not calm down he would probably hurt himself with his pent up anger lashing out at the snow and ice rocks.

Lyla overcame her sadness and fear because she cared so much for him (although up until now she had not realised quite how much) and she threw herself at him and wrapped her arms around him so tight he could not move; they both fell to the floor with Lyla still holding him tightly. Pallamo thrashed around for a while struggling and wriggling until his anger began to ebb away and he began to relax.

"please, please stop Pallamo" Lyla pleaded with him and after a while he stopped struggling all together.

"I can feel your pain Pallamo but anger never helps anything and more often than not it makes things much worse. How do you expect to help the living penguins if you are so angry because of the ones that have died" Lyla stated as though she had given the advice a million times before.

“we need all your strength and energy to help; not to cause more damage” she exclaimed in a very matter of fact tone, so that she sounded like his head mistress at school.

‘why are boys so stupid!!’ thought Lyla ‘they can only seem to express their emotions through lashing out and resorting to violence which is what’s wrong with this world. It must be something in their spirit nature from when they had to fight the dinosaurs and sabre tooth’s to protect themselves and their families and their peoples. They still had not been able to overcome their natural feelings and learnt to use their energy and passion in a better way’.

Although Lyla knew there was a better way, she still sympathised with Pallamo and realised getting upset with him would not help either of them, so she tried to reason with him and make him realise that by getting angry at bad things, he would only create more bad things in this world and especially in the spirit world where they would all go one day. Then their 'bad feeling spirit' would go into a new body and the cycle of violence and badness would grow even more. Although Lyla knew this because Orlof had sat down with her on many occasions so she would appreciate how things worked and how to make things better, she was still a little cynical herself.

"Pallamo you must learn to realise that any pain you see has become about as a price we had to pay to live in this beautiful world, through our desire to survive".

She spoke from her heart which seemed to break through to Pallamo and have a bit of an effect as though he was beginning to understand what she was going on about

"it's a part of our learning so that we can appreciate and value all the beauty there is, these dreadful things will not last long if we can overcome them quickly and we will always have a reminder of our pains and troubles we once felt, which will remind us how beautiful everything else is that we have, but we must overcome them otherwise they will overcome us and we will all be destined to a life of misery and suffering”.

It was a little too much for Pallamo to take in as he had not had such wisdom shared with him as Lyla had received from Orlof nearly every night before bed time he tried to prepare her for the path that was set before her. After a while, Lyla could see that Pallamo was beginning to feel better and he looked more positive and calm. He sat there on an ice boulder for a few minutes thinking about what Lyla had told him and asked Lyla

“So God and Mother Nature do care we just had to experience some ugly things to appreciate the beautiful things more and we have had to struggle so much and work so hard to value all the good things that we have achieved otherwise we wouldn't appreciate their value, is that what your trying to say Lyla?

"yes, yes you've nearly got it, yipeee!!!!!" Lyla whooped out loud with real joy.

"You have nearly learnt the most important lesson in life Pallamo, something that took me months and months to learn and you have learnt it in just a few minutes; Pallamo you are so clever, I love you" Lyla said and she meant it.

Pallamo was so relieved that the whole world and everything was not horrible and God and Mother Nature still cared. He thought *maybe this is why my parents argue so much, so when I'm older I will have had enough of* arguing and just want to be around people who feel good and feel joy. He felt a real joy and sense of peace in his heart which he could not remember ever having felt before and gave Lyla a hug so big it nearly crushed the breath out of her. After he let her go she picked up a huge snowball and hit him on the head and shouted:

"NOW PLEASE Let's HAVE SOME FUN TO MAKE UP FOR ALL THE PAIN THAT SURROUNDS US INSTEAD OF CREATING MORE PAIN FROM ANGER AND DESPAIR" She said before adding "THEN WE JUST MIGHT BE ABLE TO HELP AS WE WILL FEEL BETTER, WHICH WE WON'T BE ABLE TO DO IF WE GIVE IN TO PAIN AND SADNESS".

"THERE ARE LOTS OF THINGS TO DO, WE CAN RUN, JUMP, DANCE, SING AND HAVE SNOWBALL FIGHTS. THESE ARE SO MUCH BETTER THAN LASHING OUT KICKING AND YELLING. THERE ARE BETTER WAYS TO LET OUT OUR PAIN AND IF WE CAN LEARN THIS, WE WILL ALL FEEL BETTER ONE DAY AND HAVE NOTHING TO CRY FOR OR BE ANGRY ABOUT......

Then Palamo, we might be able to help the penguins….. well that's my theory, what do you say we try my friend??

When Palamo looked at her she could see in his eyes what his answer was……. and so their journey began, for real.

This was to be the beginning of a great and wonderful adventure and also started to ring true the ancient prophecy that those first Elders foresaw….

'maybe there was a prophecy after all…..' some of the local villagers started to think.

Part 2

For my family, all of ya!

After they had lay in the snow for a while, following their exhausting moment of soul searching; they got up, shook themselves off and began to climb up to the top of the cove, so that they could watch the sunset together. Pallamo started to feel quite close to Lyla, as she had opened her heart to him; and Lyla hoped that one day Pallamo could do the same for her, though she knew this would take time for him to build trust as he had so much pain in his heart. She also hoped that he would open up and be his self a little more, as for so long he had shrunk inside an invisible shell; ever since his home was broken by those terrible raiders and his parents started to argue. Lyla thought it would probably take a long time and hoped his parents would one day be able to be a good part of his life once more, maybe then he could start to heal. The sun was just reaching the horizon and it lit up some clouds a beautiful pink and red, they lay on a blanket together and let the evenings events sink in. Something really strange and exciting was happening to them both, though they were not really sure exactly what it was. It was like a whole new world was opening up before them, a world full of hope and peace and most also quite importantly happiness and joy. As they lay on the blanket that Mrs Bloomolei had given them, Pallamo wrapped his arm around Lyla to help keep her warm and to feel snug and secure with his best friend. He felt a huge sense of purpose at that moment, unlike he had ever felt before and hoped this feeling would last; as he had always felt very much alone in the world. Laying there together made all his hurt and sadness vanish for a moment and it felt like all that mattered in the whole world was looking after Lyla and making sure she was safe and happy. He hoped he could be strong and valiant enough to help her on her quest that was given her by the 'spirit family' above; which she would soon attend school for. Along with that thought, he suddenly felt a strange tingling sensation run up through his body, which seemed to come from his heart up through his shoulders and made his hairs stand on end like some kind of energy was being transferred into his soul. It gave him an overwhelming feeling of calm and love he hoped would never end; he thought it was kind of like the beautiful feeling you get when you hear a wonderful piece of music from someone with a great voice. The sun had now set, and the sky was full of the most beautiful colours that they had ever seen. Pallamo wished he was a painter so that he could paint the evening's sky so they would never forget this moment and also to show how much he cared for her.

After laying for a while, Lyla's words, she had said to him earlier ran through his mind.

‘We need a reminder of how terrible things can be so we can appreciate and value all the beauty and wonder that there is in the world and all the ‘Good Stuff’ as she called it’.

Pallamo thought that although this was probably true a little bit, he was sure that if he felt the way he did right now and just ok for the rest of the time; he would be very happy and content even without a reminder of the pain and suffering life can sometimes inflict on us. One thing he felt so sure about was that the world did not need as much misery as there was, if in fact any was needed at all. He reasoned that if this theory of Lylas was true - that some bad was needed in the world for balance and contrast - then it should be a tiny amount, as any more could destroy us all if we could not overcome it in time. If this happened then everything we had survived and worked for as human beings, would all be for nothing; and two million years of those hardships was a long time and a lot to just throw away by lack of effort and heart now. We have reached a time and place that most of humanity should feel good; if only we could only overcome the problems we had created to get here, the main one being our inability to work together; and competing against each other – which really was making things more difficult for us all in the long run.

Pallamo had learnt a lot about all the harm we had caused each other through time and all the damage we had done to our world and the creatures in it, in order to 'survive'. He had read all about the huge tribal wars of old for food and resources and also all the pain caused from religion and belief. He now realised all the harm we had caused recently in the huge world wars and from everyday greed and selfishness had caused their overall spirit and souls a huge amount of harm; so much in fact, that it hung in the balance whether or not we could overcome it. What seemed so strange to all the Eskimo people, both highly educated and lesser so, was that most of the world and nearly all people did not seem to care very much about this. This was very frightening to them all as they knew the peoples from the developed nations were not doing very much at all to help overcome the damage which after everything was quite huge and would take a massive effort on all our parts to make better. The horrifying thing was that if we did not make up for things and reverse the harm caused; then we all may suffer an eternity in 'Hell up above' which was much worse than any pain we could feel down hear '*which was quite bad enough'* Pallamo felt. Also it would last for an eternity, which he believed was quite a long time, even by Eskimos standards, who were naturally quite patient and humble.

Pallamo and Lyla suddenly felt a chill go right through them as a huge gust of wind came out of nowhere and blew across the top of the cove where they were laying together. Lyla then squeezed Pallamo tighter to keep warm and Pallamo wrapped his arm around her to protect her from the cold wind that started to blow, so that she would not freeze.

Lyla was suddenly startled as pallamo let out a large gasp of breath and bellowed out in a state of shock and excitement.

"OMG" he bellowed, before adding in a most alarming manner.

"Lyla I don't believe it!" He continued to shriek at her with huge bright wide eyes, which first looked like he had seen a ghost and then realised he had won a prize.

Lyla looked at him, both startled and a little scared, then realised he was actually excited about something; she continued to stare at him very puzzled, before he then jumped up and started jumping around still yelling 'OMG' and now doing fist pumps in the air too.

"What? What is it Pallamo? What have you seen? I really don't think you should watch any more sunsets Pallamo, this is rather silly" she said with a smile, although she was actually quite sincere too.

Her words were wasted on him as he was still leaping around like a frenzied jack in the box on Irn Bru or something.

'Why do boys have to be so crazy' Lyla thought then suddenly Pallamo took Lyla by both hands and pulled her to her feet. He gave her a huge hug before he put both his hands on his shoulders and looked deep into her eyes.

"I know how to save them" he said with true excitement and optimism

"I know how to save them Lyla" he said again, almost like he was pleading her to believe him

By this time Lyla had snapped out of her docile state before she said to him

"Pallamo what are you going on about? save who? Pallamo please calm down as your acting a bit crazy. I know things are tough for you and strange things are happening but please try and chill out and relax a little more. Who is it you can save Pallamo?"

Pallamo still gazed into Lylas' eyes with the same excited and crazy look that he did before.

"Lyla I know how to save the Penguins!!" he said exacerbated that she was not really following his thoughts or sharing his excitement and euphoria.

He was so overjoyed he felt like he could have leapt a mountain or swam the ocean. He then said it again and the next thing he did was to give her a huge big hug which swept her up off her feet and gave her a big kiss on the cheek. Lyla was quite embarrassed and a little shocked too, but she had started to let his words sink in and actually started to believe what he was saying. She started to feel a strange sense of apprehension and excitement herself. When she finally managed to push him away -as his hug was so tight she could barely breath - she could see a tear roll down his cheek. By this point Lyla knew that either everything had gotten the better of Pallamo and he was having 'a moment' of madness or perhaps he really had worked out a real way that they could save the penguins. She hoped with all her heart that it was the latter thought; as, one, she didn't want a crazy friend, and two, she loved them penguins and really did not want them all to die as it would have been a little part of her that would have died too. After Pallamo wiped away his tear, he then looked at her with such a joyful smile it made her heart flutter with happiness and Lyla could feel tears start to swell in her eyes too. After a brief moment they looked at each other with big bright smiles after they had realised how stupid they were being and suddenly began to giggle and laugh harder than they could remember... and for the briefest moment it seemed like all was right with the world.

"So?" asked Lyla when they had both calmed down and regained their composure

“How do we save em, Mr clever Clogs, if you may?”

Pallamo looked at her with his big bright brown eyes, which Lyla thought were like big sad puppy eyes, though full of care, love and kindness, but also a lot of pain.

“you just showed me how we can save them Lyla, or should I say how they can save themselves with our help”.

“When we were laying together and the wind blew, you hugged me closer to stay warm as two people together is warmer than one person on their own right?”

“Well, yes Pallamo that is quite obvious, so whats your point?” she exclaimed.

Lyla was still not thinking very well as otherwise she would have caught on by now what

Pallamo was getting at, but he continued to tell her anyway.

“Well the penguins spend all their time on their own and so they freeze”

Lylas’ eyes suddenly lit up as she then realised what he was trying to say, then she finished what he was about to say for him.

“So we have to try and get them all together?” she said with a renewed hope in her voice.

“Yes Lyla, if we can get them all to huddle together they may be able to keep warm enough over the winter”

Lyla thought it over for a few minutes then replied

“Pallamo I think it could really work as it would make them all warmer, if we can get them together; but how on earth do we get thousands of penguins to huddle together; after all, they are not renowned for their obedience or logic!"

The idea was far better than making coats for them all, that much was for sure. Lyla now felt a little daft at such a silly idea, though at the time she was a little bit tired and also a bit crazy from excitement and how fast everything was going. With Pallamo's new idea, all they had to do was to somehow try and herd the penguins together then hope they could learn to do it on their own. They both chatted about their new idea to help save the penguins and then they set off for home before it got dark.

It was a Tuesday and Lyla had forgotten that the next day, was the first day of her new term at the 'Elder school of illumination', which, along with 5 other hopeful children, is where Lyla was lucky enough to be chosen to study. Lyla loved the 'Elder lessons', a hundred times more than her normal school where the classes were too big for them to chat or discuss anything properly. Her new 'Elder Lessons were calm and relaxing. Lyla loved them because she got to have some really good chats and debates with just a few other pupils so was easy to pay attention. As Lyla was so advanced in her learning she also found her old classes boring and too easy. She hoped she would pass this year and be accepted as a full time 'Elder' pupil, as that would make her parents so proud and she would feel amazing to be able to one day hopefully help guide the future of all the villages in the district. This would mean that Lyla would be responsible for the future health and well-being of all her friends and family and also everyone else. This really appealed to Lyla as for as long as she could remember she had thought that there was a lot of things that could be improved in the area and she had a lot of ideas that she thought could really help improve things for everyone; even that annoying oaf Malakei, who she loathed as he was sometimes quite mean. She would actually even help him; as she was taught that it is the responsibility of all society, the way in which any one individual feels and consequently acts (*see my poem Us and them). This is because, from the start of our time here on earth, we have all been a part of both the bad and the good and all the badness that has been created through our acts, is a result of our need for survival. This meant it is actually the planet and nature, which is mostly the cause of the badness that has grown from the start of mankind. This is our price we have had to pay to be able to enjoy all the wonders that there are here. It is now all our responsibility to make everything better on earth, so we can overcome all this badness and suffering we have endured for so long now. Lyla knew we had learnt and built so much, that it was possible for everyone to have a good life. She knew that we now had to learn to put each other first – which was contrary to our natural instincts – in order to reverse the badness that had grown from living for ourselves for so long. This was the key to healing and the doorway to happiness and stability. Lyla had learnt that every living thing with a body and mind was a part of the 'family of mankind' and ultimately a part of the same spirit; this thought sometimes made Lyla feel quite ill knowing that she was not only related to but also a part of Malakei as he was a part of her, albeit an extended and temporarily detached part. One time when Lyla thought of this she was actually a little bit sick in her mouth and was very close to vomiting. She did not even feel so bad when she realised that she was also of the same origin as the chimpanzees that sat around all day picking their bums and noses and doing rolly pollies. Lyla really hoped that she could one day feel better and more tolerant towards things she didn't like; as she knew she could sometimes be too dismissive and lacking empathy, though she had her limits and was not perfect by any stretch of the imagination. All she could do was to work very hard to make herself as considerate and understanding as possible and to look after herself as best she could, by means of a healthy diet, exercise, relaxation and reflection, good sleep, fun and enjoyment in moderation; and also Gods greatest gift, of, giving as much as she could spare and finding joy in other people's happiness (which was easier now she realised everyone was a part of the same spirit. Doing her best with these virtues meant she had peace in her heart and would one day be able to leave the world with a clear conscience. Although she hoped she could be better, she also hoped that Malakei would stop being such an oaf and change a little too, so that she would not have to be a saint to put up with him.

When Lyla and Pallamo started to walk home, they had to pass by all the dead penguins again, which brought back some of the sombre feelings they had earlier; though they now felt better about the situation and they promised each other that they would not rest for a minute until they had stopped the needless suffering that lay beside them right before their eyes. This kind of suffering was so different from things they had seen on the news or 'you tube' at Orions cabin. as this was close by and they could feel and see the pain with their very own hearts and with their very own eyes. This made it much harder to ignore or wanted to help which is the very essence of all of our natures – to protect each other - when we search deep enough and peel back the layers and years of the armour that we have built up since our beginning. This was how they both felt, however at the back of their mind they both wondered if they really could do anything to help save the penguins. After all, they were just two young children and if the adults could not save them, then how on earth could they? Even with Lylas wisdom and Pallamos bag of stuff, it was still a massive task to undertake. This doubting kept Lyla awake for most of the night, before she remembered that, a little bit of worry was good, but too much was terribly bad. So instead of worrying any longer she thought of laying in the cove with Pallamo and watching the beautiful sunset together, this feeling of love and friendship overcame her worrying and soon Lyla drifted off to a deep and peaceful sleep.

The next morning the sun shone through Lylas window and woke her up earlier than usual, she felt really tired still after her adventures with Pallamo the day before and wished she could stay in bed. The sun was shining bright and she felt a real sense of hope and positivity in her heart. It felt like the first day of spring after a winter so long that everyone had forgotten what it was like to have sunshine and new life. It really felt like things were changing, perhaps it may have been that Lyla was going to be approaching her 'teenage years' in the not too distant future, which Geomei told her would have huge effects on her emotions and feelings and she may get all crazy and unstable, as she started to make the transition from child to adult. Lyla thought it could be that, but something deep in her core felt that it was not just her, but that significant changes were happening in the environment all around her.

Orloff knocked on her bedroom door carrying a large tray of food, it had all her favourite stuff, as Orloff had made an extra effort because it was her first day of her new term. There was 'egg soldiers', a big bowl of muesli and also her favourite smoothie. The igloo they lived in was one of the best in the village and Lyla loved it so much she did not think that she could ever live in another because it was filled with memories of such joy and happiness and love, that the thought of living anywhere else made her feel actually quite homesick. Their home was not remarkable in any way; it did not have a lot of expensive and decorative things and was actually quite simple in terms of furniture and belongings. It did however, have years of care and love poured into it and everything in it had a great feeling of character and charm. Both Orloff and Geomei spent a long time making sure that every piece of furniture and every ornament had a sentiment that reflected humility and kindness. It was a home like most old people have and a bit like going to visit the best grandparents in the world, though with some really cool stuff too. They had both settled down early and were also both of similar mentality when it came to caring and looking after things. This did not mean it was outdated and old fashioned, even though many of the things in it were old, it was just that because they looked after everything so well and also kept things fitting with the time, that it all worked together. They had many modern things also which complimented the things they already had. Their home was the heart of the village and you could literally feel the warmth and love that exuded from its own personality it seemed to have. This was Orloff and Geomei's passion - having a place where everyone could come and feel good and relax. Their home always had a visitor of some sort and there was not usually a night gone by when Lylas friends were not hanging about, sometimes even when Lyla was not there. Every kid in the village thought of Orloff and Geomei as an Uncle and Aunt and would often get them birthday and Christmas cards which said Uncle Orloff or Auntie Geomei. Not only was it a great home but it also was always shining as it had different coloured twinkle lights hanging around it all year long. They even had a room which was filled with the most amazing things; from a box of magic tricks to science sets and craft making things like a pottery wheel. Orloff and Geomei never got a moment to themselves, which is exactly the way they wanted it. For a long time they had only felt joy through the happiness of others and seldom done anything purely for their own pleasure. This was also why they were so madly in love with each other, not because they fancied the pants off each other but because they shared gods greatest gift with sincerity and purity, together it created a beacon of light so bright Lyla was sure it could be seen from outer space and little did she know that she was not far wrong; which she was soon to find out.

After Lyla got home from her first Elder lesson (***which we will find out all about in the full novel*), which was mostly just an introduction to the class and an ice breaker, she went to fetch Pallamo and Orloff to go and help the penguins. They collected some rations (they would normally call this food but as seen as it was not an epic adventure and quest, rations felt more befitting). After they bid farewell to geomei they set off for the cove with hope in their hearts and determination in their spirit. As they reached the top of the cove the sadness grew once more in their hearts as they saw all the dead penguins. Lyla could feel pallamo's feelings begin to change so she quickly took his hand and said to him.

"C'mon Pallamo, if we stand here all day feeling sad we will lose even more of them

With that he shook himself off and nodded his head before a little smile grew on his face. They then ran off towards the penguins and started waving and shouting. At first the penguins all ran in different directions but after a while (following Lyla's…erm I mean pallamos brilliant plan). The penguins started to huddle together and after a short while soon looked happier and more positive. The kids ran around the penguins in a circle to keep them all together and then after a while they started to walk back up the cove.

Pallamos' idea was a success and although it took them ages to get the penguins to huddle togetherit seemed to have workd. After watching the penguins for a few hours they could see that they were beginning to look healthier and more lively, this filled their hearts with more joy than they had ever felt before.

After a few weeks since they had managed to get the penguins to huddle together, there were only a few penguins dying each week. Lyla thought that this could not be helped as all the penguins tried to get to the centre of the huddle and inevitably the smaller weaker penguins on the outside would start to freeze. It was only a few and they were all happy that it was better than the 20 or 30 that had perished each week before they had managed to help them.

The joy they felt however, did not last long. They calculated that after a few months an average of 5-6 penguins would die each week, which over a year was still quite a significant amount. One evening as the best friends lay together upon the cove, along with Orloff, Lyla suddenly had a horrific thought.

"If this many penguins are dieing each week and there is only a thousand or so in the group; then at the end of the year the group will reduce by around a third. This will mean that there won't be as much heat and more will start to die and eventually the group will shrink and shrink until their all dead"

After watching the penguins for the last few weeks with such hope, and feeling a huge amount of responsibility and care towards them; as they had directly intervened with their natural habitat and altered their living conditions; the realisation was too much for Lyla to take and she was truly heart-broken at the thought. After everything they had been through and the euphoria they had all felt, this terrible news made all their joy and hope vanish in a single instant. They had not saved the penguins as they had thought just a few moments ago, but instead they had just prolonged their suffering. They camped out at the top of the cove over the next few nights along with Orloff, as a way of mourning the penguins before they would return home and get on with their normal lives again.

After their second night out, in the early hours of the morning the sun broke the horizon of the cove and the light woke them from their fitful and light sleep. It was a beautiful sunset and they watched the sun rise until it shone down on the group of penguins. They were all huddled together and they could see the little ones on the outside of the group slowly freezing to death. Their sense of despair and hopelessness was so overwhelming that they all sat their numb with grief and tears rolling down their cheeks as their hearts let out some of the pain they were feeling. After a few minutes of sitting there in silence and feeling worse than they could ever remember, they all looked up at the horizon and saw the sun fully breach the top of the horizon, as though the earth had somehow let it go free into the sky. It was one of the most beautiful sunrises they had ever seen and the sky was full of the most gorgeous pastel colours of orange and pinks reflecting off the clouds. Witnessing such beauty and such horror at the same time made them all feel quite ill at the thought of it. "Why must there be such tragedy in this world when there is so much beauty?" Pallamo expressed exasperated with the situation, tbefore adding.

"surely there must be a way to make things better, as something that makes you feel so ill and repulsed, must not belong in a place that has so much wonder as well!. This sentiment made them all feel quite uneasy and it was lucky they had seen the magnificent sunset or they all would have been in a truly sad state, probably for quite some time. After a while of sitting there feeling truly sickened at natures cruelty and darkness Orloff finally broke the silence and shared a sentiment he himself had found hard to swallow as a young boy.

“My dear children, although it is very hard to take; this is the way of this world.... it is full of bitter-sweet moments and things that sometimes make you feel sick to the core but it is also filled with things that sometimes make your heart full of such love and joy that nothing else matters. It is best to try and accept the bad my dears and change it through nurture, influence and kindness, otherwise you will never have peace in your heart and you will miss what goodness there is”

Orloffs words did little to lift the moods of the two children, although deep down they knew he was right, though they also felt beyond any miniscule of a doubt that things were not meant to be quite so awful; certainly not in this day and age! This thought was compounded by their spirits and deep in their hearts as they suddenly felt an unyielding and resolute sense of righteousness and they both knew then that things must get better and get better quickly before it was too late!

Orloff sensed the children's desire and he tried to comfort them a little and appease them by also telling them that

"There is much beauty, love and kindness in the world and with this there also needs to be some suffering and cruelty, it's just the way of the universe and is needed to have balance. There are both light and darkness everywhere my children, and one day you will learn this, it is better if we try and stay focused on the light and do not be overcome by the darkness".

The next thing that happened both shocked and startled Orloff, as precisely the same time the children both let out a loud distressing cry and suddenly got up and ran down the cove towards the penguins. At first Orloff could not really comprehend what was happening but as he heard their cries he felt their pain and anguish to his very core and it reverberated and passed through him up above for all the angels to hear and the spirit world beyond. In that moment they both cried out all the pain and suffering that they had ever felt and they both completely lost control. The next thing Orloff knew was that the kids had suddenly started to run with all their strength and speed they could muster down towards the penguins. As they reached the bottom of the cove, near to where the penguins were, it looked for a few seconds like they were literally floating through the air. Perhaps the angels had heard their cries and had carried them aloft in their wings to the stricken penguins. When they reached them, they both cried out in despair yelling:

"STOP!!, GOD PLEASE STOP THIS PLEASE!!, Please God, there does not need to be such suffering. This is wrong and we are sorry we have let things get so bad, please help us to stop them suffering so badly!! This is so terrible and there can be goodness and beauty without all this pain and death. Please help us find a way god!! Please!!"

With that, the children fell down next to the penguins sobbing in the snow until they had let out all their grief and anguish and all that could be heard was a gentle whimpering coming from there cold and tired bodies. At first Orloff was very concerned and nearly ran down to the children but then he thought he would just let them deal with things in their own time. What really surprised Orloff was the fact that all the penguins stayed in the same place even when the children reached them. He thought this must be because they were so cold and maybe too tired to react but there was something else he could not quite explain, something almost magical. Then, even more to Orloffs surprise, he actually did see something magical a miracle even, at first he thought his eyes were playing tricks on him but after he wiped his eyes he realised he was seeing something truly wonderful.

As the children lay sobbing next to the penguins the stronger adult penguins in the centre of the group must have heard their cries of pain as they slowly started shuffling out from the centre to investigate what was causing such a harrowing and distressing call. As the larger penguins reached the outside the younger weaker penguins had worked their way to the centre where they started to recover from the freezing temperatures. From the top of the cove Orlof could see that the larger adults then looked almost shocked at the site of all the younger dead penguins, on the outside of the group and for the next few hours they all stayed on the outside until the little ones got warmer. The strong adults then seemed to shuffle about on the outside as though they were discussing what to do. Although Orlofs fatherly instincts were to go down to the children and comfort them he waited a while so that he wouldn't affect the natural behaviour of the adult penguins. After a few more minutes Lyla and Palamo got up from the freezing ground and slowly made their way back up the cove. They were both absolutely frozen and quite delirious by the time they reached him but when he pointed down to the penguins they seemed to get a supernatural energy from the spirits as they stopped shaking and stood there in awe watching the beautiful penguins start to save each other and ultimately themselves. The children then turned to Orlof, almost trying to confirm what they were seeing. As they both looked at him they noticed a look in Orlofs eyes, which was like all the heavens in the universe were looking out through them from deep within his soul. Then for the first time ever since she arrived in this world Lyla saw a tear roll down his cheek. As they both looked at him they could not see sadness, but a really strange smile that they did not really know what emotion it was, as they had never felt it in their hearts before, what they were feeling now. It was so powerful that they both suddenly felt like the most powerful souls on the planet and like nothing could ever hurt them. It was like all the wonderful emotions rolled into one, Joy, Love, Hope, Wonder etc. But there was something else something they could not describe as no words had been invented yet. Both Lyla and Palamo then turned again towards the penguins, looking down at them with that most wonderful of feelings in their *heart* and they all stood there to cherish the moment until they could stand there no longer.

They had not only witnessed something truly wonderful, but for the first time since arriving here on earth, living creatures that were not human, had risked sacrificing themselves for fellow creatures that were not directly linked or closely related. They had stood there watching in awe for so long that they could not feel their bodies, so Orlof said to the children that they really must go home, but he knew that no words or actions were going to be able to tear them away any time soon. After they had stood there for a while longer there was suddenly a moment of intense anxiety as they watched the larger penguins make their way to the centre once again. They all held their breaths watching to see what would happen, they were all literally petrified the adults would stay in the centre again; but they need not had worried, as after much hooting and chirping from the penguins they all started shuffling around every few hours until darkness came. They had all watched with the humblest and grateful appreciation and were truly grateful that they had the privilege of seeing such a beautiful act of kindness and selflessness, that it made their heart ache at the thought. They could have stayed there all night long to watch those most funny and beautiful of Gods creatures; but Orlof started to become seriously worried about their own temperature and after much persuasion, he convinced the children to leave and start their way towards home....

As they were trudging through the snow towards their village, both Pallamo and Lyla new that Lyla's feelings about something changing around them was true; they then both took hold of Orlofs hand and trudged back towards their beautiful village, looking forward to some hot chocky and marshmallows and they both wondered what on earth would happen next....they could not wait and tell Geomei and the rest of the village and they could not wait to see the penguins again...those most wonderful and daft creatures who we share our home with. Our Home.

Authors note:

Look forward to the full novel which I hope to release later this year. If you have bought the basic version from amazon before this one then please facebook me with a message and a pic of the book and I will send you some goodies as a way of compensation and gratitude (hopefully by then I will have a home and somewhere to write 'better'!!).

If my books are successful I am gonna pay for somewhere to live and if they are very successful I shall help my family. After this I hope to use any other profits from this series and autobiographies and art to buy some land to build a 'home' for the disadvantaged (mostly the Elderly, Homeless and Youngsters from deprived areas – with things for them to do) I shall give more information about this work later in the series. (secretly build a cult and make crafts to get some water to our African family...can't believe after all this time most don't have clean water ☹)

Thank you so much for your support and kindness.

Motivation and Inspiration:

All characters and work in this book are purely fictional and any likeness to any real person is purely coincidence and probably down to many people being able to relate in some way to the many points that are made about the way we live. I myself sometimes feel lacking, both ethically and pragmatically after reading the book (because me life so ruddy hard) and I hope I can one day live my life true to the sentiment that the book is about; I also hope it can help you too a little in some way.

Although the work is purely fiction, I have had first-hand experience of many of the philosophical theories; and I am especially sure without a matter of a doubt about the fact that we all have a soul/spirit of some sort which will carry on long after our time here on earth and also that all the energy here is a part of the same entity. Much of this has been proven to a certain extent and is commonly accepted in nearly all religions and faiths and also by most world academic experts and scientists.

My own journey:

Many of the sentiments and ethical points within this book are from my own personal experiences and those of some wonderful people I have met along the way.

Since I was a young lad, who had to survive very humble and trying beginnings in an area of quite extreme poverty and deprivation; I have spent much of my time trying to come up with ways to help resolve conflict and improve the quality of life for people. I have spent nearly the last 20 years committed to this work and I have found myself having been part of an incredible journey. From assisting British dignitaries in Afghanistan, watching the Aurora in Iceland with the most amazing person and inspiration I have met; to watching meteor showers with complete strangers, handing out pens and pencils to kids in India, to sleeping rough on the streets for several years and being bed ridden (critically ill) and staying with loved ones, right here in the UK just last year having been driven to alcohol for some time on and off since childhood.

I looked at my facebook pics the other day and it looks like I have had the most amazing life ever, this is far from true. I was quite healthy and felt ok for a few months whilst in the Army (the rest was very hard work building my health and growing as a person) the rest of the time I have mostly felt quite numb inside and apart from a few thrills from time to time at festivals or on holiday etc; I have mostly felt pretty crud. I have learnt a lot though and I am persevering with healing so I can feel better inside and then hopefully physically again too, though I don't have my hopes to high, the walk has certainly been a good start though. I hopeI can find the decent quality of life (housing, work, social life etc) to enable me to sustain the benefits of the hard work I put in...

It really has been a rollercoaster which feels like I have lived a hundred lives in one go. The journey has been incredibly arduous and testing at times with great highs and extreme and prolonged lows. Sadly, the lows have outweighed the highs a hundred fold (though I hope that 'balance' is trying to put that right). I have however had some truly wonderful moments, felt some miraculous things and have met and spent time with some remarkable and wonderful human beings. So thank you so much to all those people. It goes without saying I have met a few dragons along the way ;-), which comes with the territory I have ventured down, though I really feel that even the scariest had some goodness that was driving them, I just hope those who have not been a positive part of my life and others like me, will one day feel better and see things differently which is up to us all really. Looking back now, would I put myself through all the trauma and despair if I had known just how badly it would have got? NO WAY!!! Haha, and this is not just me trying to be humble or modest or cute, I really wouldn't. If I had known of all the hardships, I could not possibly let myself – or anyone for that matter – go through so much pain, (which I am going through still, as I am still sleeping rough though things are getting better and I have turned my own misfortune into an adventure as I explained). I truly think that one individual should not go through so much suffering in one lifetime, though I do feel that a little bit of suffering can actually be good from time to time; perhaps self-inflicted is better than from others or generally from life. Having said that, perhaps I will feel differently in years to come. I also hope with all my heart that people will continue to take big risks in life for what matters most in their hearts; as long as it's for positive and healthy change to help improve life and not harm it of course. I hope people will continue to push the boundaries in the name of positive and healthy change; after all I think this is what makes us human (caring for one another as much as ourselves). The most important thing I hope you take from this book is this:

Having learnt the things I have, and feeling the way I do now, this sometimes makes me feel bad about the way I treated people and lived my life before I learnt to *RECYCLE which I havn't quite mastered yet ;-).* When I read my writings back from time to time I still feel very lacking and sometimes quite horrified by the way I had to live and the world I was born into and it saddens me still that so many of us still have to. The point I am trying to make is that, in essence, we are all just a part of one big pool of energy (our actions), these actions have meant sometimes being quite terrible to each other because of our need to fight for food and resources as we have grew and evolved. This energy is just passed around from one another and also to our environment which we may look after or not, as a consequence. Until the last few decades most of us have dealt with the bad feelings with ever more destructive ways to console ourselves, so those bad feelings are made worse and passed on. What lyla learns in one of her Elder lessons (coming soon in the 'Full Novel' If they find me somewhere decent to work that is) is that we can actually recycle that bad energy, firstly by using the feeling it gives us to help others within our community – take out our ill feeling by mending a fence or shopping for an OAP or something similar and then doing something healthier for ourselves and treating ourselves…. – although we do not naturally feel like doing such things; we mostly want to console ourselves or take our aggression out on someone else; if we do positive things afterwards, such as exercise or a healthy and constructive recreational activity like climbing or dancing etc, then we soon feel much better. Sadly for a long time we have chosen to take out our woes by excess; food, shopping, alcohol, drugs or Morris Dancing ;-)

(obviously the most destructive). Hence, because of this culture and mentality we have all made each other, our planet and probably our pets and fellow creatures too, feel much much worse. The thing is, until now, we have known no better ways, so although I still feel bad when I look back and wished I could have lived a better life, I now know this is stupid and holding me back from living the life that I am now responsible for, much more so than before, with this new knowledge and tool that I have learnt from Uni (took a while though but thanks haha☺). I really hope I can improve my lifestyle and work to keep myself feeling good and healthy so that I can pass on good feeling, as I do also hope one day we can all learn to do this, even just a little bit. Who knows what our world will bless us with then, if we can, as it blesses us with so much already; when we just slow down and take a moment to look around us as ourselves and then with others.

Ps I planned to walk 5 thousand miles (though this has turned into around 10,000 miles and I am planning 24,000 to commemorate the great acheivements of our scientists landing on the moon.for charities including The Salvation Army and Help for Heroes, pictures of which can be found on my Facebook page Johno Johnson – linked to the page underneath.

Thanks to everyone for everything who has helped along the way, especially my close friends and family!!!

Check out my website and pages ☺:

https://darrengregjohnson4.wixsite.com/thepenguinstheory

https://www.facebook.com/ThePenguinsTheoryArt/

https://www.facebook.com/The-Penguins-Theory-358227477895102/

or email me: darren.greg.johnson40@gmail.com

The Penguins Theory Poems.

By D G Johnson

The following writings are a collection of Poems and descriptions, inspired and written during my long walk (sabbatical adventure) which fit in with the book and my work.

In March 2015 I was critically ill and suffered what I can only describe as a quite severe heart attack. I am not sure what it was exactly (a heart attack of some sort) but for about 3 days I was bed ridden and could barely move without feeling a very severe pain in my heart, 'it was like a knife had been plunged into it', would be how I would describe the excruciating pain. I was mostly in tears and thought I would croak it at any moment. My heart goes out to my Mum and sister and other family members who must have been terribly saddened and worried I was in such dire health. Anyhoo, I survived and went off on a little adventure so as not to let my life be the cause of more worry or despair (by being in their life ill) from my loved ones.

I am not sure what caused the severe pain exactly; my life was in a terrible state and I was mixing with the 'undesirables' as a way to show some kind of immature rebellion or something (if truth be told, I seemed to have little other choice) perhaps it was a bit of both; having little choice and no inclination to make things better (I was very hurt and broken hearted – from this world in general). I may have been poisoned or even injured during a night of being over intoxicated or drugged – not sure! Maybe it was just that I was smoking and drinking too much and this was God's way of saying you have to do something different (if so he could have just sent me on a campsite and gave me a reasonable quality of life – perhaps he wanted me to go on a 'mega adventure sabbatical' including an epic walk of around 10,000 miles, who knows?) anyway what happens in life happens, rightly or wrongly and you can either spend the rest of your life looking back and let the event hurt you much more or you can go off wandering around and see what you find, if you have no money that is; otherwise go and do some fun stuff, there's lots to do when you have money and quite a bit to do even when you don't.

I went off and I found some amazing things I want to share with you....

The first poem is a tribute to Rudyard Kipling who wrote one of my all- time favorite poems called 'If'. It is a remarkable poem and a great 'life guide'. My Dad often tried to instill the virtues of the poem into me and I guess that to live your life well – in this day and age - it's hard to remember all the advice parents give you; a poem is an easy way to remember some....if you can remember it that is!

I was making quite good recovery, although very bored living with my sister as I had no job, money or much to do. So I decided to write a poem to honor Rudyards and to say thanks to my Dad on father's day and to show him after all, how much he meant to me and everything he did to try and be a good Dad and role model; though I realize it was terribly hard for him.

At this time, I was very ill and fragile.... over the last year or so I had probably consumed enough alcohol to keep the Engalnd Football, Rugby and cricket fans going for the rest of the decade and given and spiked with 'god only knows' what illicit drugs whilst under the influence. I had also turned 'strict vegetarian' overnight and had been under huge amounts of stress from study, relations and various lovely people for a very long time.

I did not feel like socializing much with family as I felt so fragile and was very depressed so did not want to bring them down so if I was not out walking - I realised this was the only simulative healthy thing I could do, with how I was feeling – I was stuck in my sister spare room (which had no TV or other entertainment – mean gits I thought at the time – though they probably did not want me to end up a recluse) I had exhausted my game of 'keep the feather in the air' (my nephew looked really concerned when he came in to check on me one day…sorry Ade!! I hope to make it up to you ☺) The game was quite a simple and (to be honest not very exciting or healthy) fun way to pass an hour. I found a feather and learnt that by waving my hands above it very fast I could keep it in the air…think I managed about 30 secs!!! Wooohooo……………Sorry, If you still have the will to live let me get back to the point. I started to get really bored of the same walks and so I started to write a little. Although it sounds very forthright and wise, I was trying to re-teach myself the virtues that the poem intended and I by no means was in a position of how best to live. The first line was something that I really had to instill in myself as I knew I had been through a lot and I did not want to end up mean or hard. It's about realizing that although we are all so very different we are all in this together and where one ends up and how one feels, we will all one-day end up feeling the same and that we are all a part of each other's feelings through our hearts and spirit. I hope to explain how I came to this conclusion but if you shut yourself away for a few weeks make yourself a little fragile somehow (no meat or something....) and open your heart, you will probably feel the same if you can be honest with yourself, although your life may not let you! (if it's a tough life).

If again... (A tribute to Rudyard kipling)

If you can learn to love, everyone the same

If you can relate with others, about hope, not blame

If you can listen to your heart, when your really not sure

If you can use your senses, but not trust them too much

If you can learn to master, your emotions with faith

If you can learn to recycle, for a much better place*

If you can make yourself strong and not become numb

If you can find courage through beauty, and help it to grow

NOT with force nor fear, but inspiring it sow

If you can be kind to all creatures as well as yourself

If you can believe in something, and protect it, with hearts desire

Be happy and healthy like a bird on a wire

If you can live for the living, but not condemn all who's lost

For a life for the living, comes at such a high cost

If you find offence in what others may do, then maybe they need someone like you!

So give all you can and keep a little in reserve

Help build a bright future and do keep your nerve

Imagine that we, are all part of a whole, every living creature, both big and both small

If you can take your share and give back a little more, it shall be returned of this we are sure

So keep living how you wish, for your children to live

So one day they can be, someone like you...

What we are trying to say, through our tears of life...

Is that we are proud what you're doing

And all that you do!!

*Recycling bad energy into good. Penguins Theory!

The first line – I'm still trying, God give me strength!!

The second line is important for me, as its so easy – when you've had a crap ride and tough times, or feel insecure or lacking – to focus on people or things that you think (or want to be) worse than you – I still do ☹. So many of us do this so we can relate with each other and feel better about ourselves, which is a sad reflection on the state we are all in. I have found myself doing this a lot of times in my life and feel pretty crud I was not able to just try and improve my life or myself. This was not always possible though and I know it isn't for many, especially if you have responsibilities such as kids, mortgage etc. I sadly did not have many responsibilities (apart from my family, I grew up with) so I am one of the worst culprits ☹ I am trying to make up for this now though and have for quite a while so hopefully, it is hard to focus our negative energy on hope though I hope I can help teach you this amazing tool and gift, when I have mastered it myself that is!

What else do I drone on about in the poem....:-)....!!

Ok without writing an essay and fear of being a cause of more negativity in this world....I mention about using your heart when you're not sure. I remember a saying from school that if you know something well 'you know it off by heart' this is very true; much of what we learn sinks in to our 'being' and even when we cannot remember what is right or wrong to do, we can feel it in our heart. This helps if your life is very stressful, though be careful as your heart can be fooled – especially if you're a sad and lonely git like me.

I then go on to mention 'recycling' which I'm sure your all well and truly bored with by now, so I will go onto the next verse I find to be of some significant worth:

'If you can make yourself strong
and not become numb'

To me, now, in this day and age and with the life I have had (its been trying at best) this is one of the most important sentiments I want to try and express. If you have a hard life, in whatever way, then you can either do one of two things: numb yourself to whatever it is your finding difficult (pain, work, relations, fear, yourself, etc) with distraction (food, drink, drugs, sex etc) or you can make yourself strong (usually exercise, gym, sport, mediation etc) the problem is that if we make ourselves too strong and in the wrong way its very easy to become numb (hard hearted) and not feel all the good things...(so many I don't have time......). I think I have found a middle ground though it really depends on the person and also the life they have. I hope that I can give some pointers though so that you can use them as a guide and adjust to your own needs (what works best for you).

What else......

Ahhh,

'If you can find courage through beauty, and help it to grow

NOT with force nor fear, but inspiring it sow'.

On my walk and during my many years of nobody wanting to be around me very much, in a social way - as I was a highly strung, insecure, neurotic dick, I took some time to reflect on a few things and I soon came to realise that possibly and probably nearly all progress (in terms of development and civilization) was mostly achieved under some sort of duress. I think these factors, have also meant that we have not been able to enjoy the great and wonderful things we have made, quite so much. I think something happens in our spirit when we are forced to do things, even if we want to do the things anyway – I think we have rebelious ickle spirits and they get all upset when they are forced to do things. This verse above is about trying to inspire development and progress, purely for the joy of doing it, instead of 'modern day force' via having to pay the rent etc. If we can find the beauty of giving and the joy it brings when we open our hearts then maybe we could create much more breathtaking and amazing things, which we would all enjoy so much more. A rather idealistic and profound notion one suspects, (I've always wanted to say 'one in that way) but who knows maybe it's a way of living we could work towards, as there are probs far too many lazy gits like me in this day and age so we would make very little progress and not get anywhere without 'motivating factors' such as the need to pay for shelter and food.

Sorry I got a little bored of writing about me poems but will write more about them later on me facebook pages ☺

*Us and them (as described).

I woke up in a hedgerow, looking into big brown eyes,
I tell you what I saw in them caught me by surprise,
twas not contempt nor fury, as I would have felt so,
just a smidgen of bewilderment and a little bit of sorrow.

I found myself just quite perplexed, those eyes do not condemn us,
the harm and pain we've done to them, they've somehow let it go.

A feeling grew inside me, one that I'd not felt,
In such a very long time, when ice started to melt.

I felt the deepest sadness, at who I had become,
Who was to blame for all this pain,
It must have been someone.

I searched this fiendish fellow, up high and down below,
Why did he have to be so mean, I really had to know.
I found so many suspects, it must be one of them,
Looking quite despicable, I started to condemn.

I punished and I hollered, until I had no more,
I gave all that I had and heaven knew what for.
I took a breath and looked within, to see if we were healing,
But to my horror, what I saw, was rather quite displeasing.

I had not stopped the pain they caused, but only made it worse.
I suddenly then realised where all this hurt came from,
It was not simply only them, but a little bit of us.

By Darren Greg Johnson 06/2016

Adversity and Spirit.

This worlds shown much adversity,
Its pushed us to our limits.
Swimming, crawling, climbing up
Thank goodness for our spirit.

When dusk would settle and we had no more,
We would find a strength within.

Connected to something,
so powerful, so pure, so true,
By heart's desire we carried on,
with chances few and thin.

We found a way when hope was gone,

Disease and famine and war.
Oh curse that darkness we came across,
Heaven knows what for?

Blessed are we with fortitude,
To strengthen and nourish our soul.

As the bell tolls, our final hour,
adversity will know,
we staggered on,
we stooped so low;

But we made this world, our home

Our forgotten family

How did they keep their faith and spirit,

being pushed and pushing themselves beyond limits.

Oh what despair, terror and grief,

they must have felt, quite beyond belief.

Those trenches, rats and lice their home,

soaked to the depths, chilled to the bone.

These things but just, gods fraught distraction,

to cloud the bullet and dull the blade,

as they pierce the heart of our human spirit,

each ounce of pain, dragging us deeper,

into darkness that madness grows,

until we lose ourselves and lose our soul.

What do we become after horrors of war,

we all lose something, of this I am sure.

So now we have found a place we once lost,

buried beneath blood and gore,

In the dirt and earth, of our blessed new home,

With enough for all and one true faith,

In ourselves, our friends and the family we lost.

By Darren Greg Johnson 02/1017

Sword and shield

What is my heart for, they ask to me.
Alas, it is my sword and my shield, I say,
the love I feel can shield me from pain,
And the joy and kindness, can, likewise
cut through darkness,
It is our essence and being and
connection to each other and God;
Though it is long buried, deep, under
layers of hardships, that we've endured
whilst making this harsh and cruel world
our home.

But fear no longer my good friends, for
we have appeased Mother Nature in this
place of wonder and she is starting to
share her beauty and offer her jewels.
But we must respect her, I beseech you
this, for she can suddenly turn; and the
comforts and joy we have earned can so
easily be taken, if she wishes; we can be
thrown into the abyss of space and time

in a much poorer state than when we arrived and this hell can last such a great length of time.

So let us worship and praise her and look after her so, as she looks after us all; for she is our home and whilst we are here she is in our hearts. So with our shield lets protect her and let's cast more light upon her with our sword.

Let us rejoice with her, for we still have some heart and spirit and she shall return much more than we gave, as long as we have faith in her and respect her.

Darren Greg Johnson 14/11/16

The Penguins Theory, is something when,

We all take turns, to give again.

The joy of giving I'm sure you'll find,

In your heart something kind.

A happiness you felt before,

To raise a smile

And nothing more.

Its where magic happens,

wonders grow,

Its our new world,

lets build it so.

The way you want,

As a child before,

When things were new

And feelings pure.

Lets lift ourselves,

Out of this rut,

Some time away,

From Orions hut.

To sing again, run,

skip and jump,

Climbing up,

Out of this slump.

Recycling is quite rather simple;

Use badness that you feel inside,

For something good,

Something kind.

Then treat yourself

Do something fun

Recycling it, has now begun.

Dance as though,

You just don't care

Go spoil yourself

We're getting there!

You've just recycled bad to good

The Penguins Theory

We really should

By Darren Greg Johnson 03/2017

Changing Skies

I have walked a long way, under changing skies, beneath the flight and song.
An acorn falls and sits a while, though never sits for long.
Underneath the undergrowth, an ancient world appears,
Sliding, crawling, leaping by, that I'd not seen for years.

How I forgot there's more to us, than always meets the eye,
How I forgot we've grown so much, as the years go by.

I lay beneath the magnolia tree and beauty overcomes,
Peering up amongst its blossom, to stare into the sun.
Clouds shift and shape, connecting with, and moving me inside;
A feeling like I used to know, when home was far and wide.

How close we are and yet so far, away from toil and blood;
The earth beneath, turning with, all our pain and love.
The stars shine through the atmosphere, seeing how we are;
What would they do, if only they knew, we

have gone way too far.
Our galaxy surrounds us, the ship we sail upon;
I wonder where she's going, I wonder where
we're from.

I have walked a long way, under changing skies,
Seen hunger, famine, war; courage kindness
and more,
Though what I will take with me, I never really
saw.

And too leave you with and to bid you farewell and thanks.

It is only when we look up, as our small vulnerable selves, that we start to appreciate the beauty and wonder of our life and world. Seeing the moon, stars and galaxy and feeling it in our heart and spirit puts things into perspective really how things are:

We are just spirits in bodies inhabiting a tiny, tiny round rock full of a gargantuan amount of curiosities; looking out of two eyes from a million different perspectives, during our time here on this wonderful rock, spinning amongst the vastness of an eternal space with all its possibilities...

Thankl you so much for buyinh my book it is obviously not that great and I need to spend a lot of time making it better, though sadly as I am scraping by trying to get commissions on the high street most of the day I have little time.

Please keep an eye on my facebook pages:

Darren Greg Johnson Artist

Darren Greg Johnson Poet

And email darrengregjohnson100@gmail.com

Printed in Great Britain
by Amazon

56975497R00106